Cure for the Common Killer

Salvatore Iaquinta, MD

To good intentions.

Chapter 1

I looked at my on-call phone's caller ID. Extension 1138. The emergency room. Great way to start my morning at work.

I flipped it open...perhaps the last flip phone on the planet, if not here in this small hospital in Oakland, California. "Hello?"

"Rees? It's Vivian. Can you get down here ASAP? I think this lady is losing her airway."

Normally I would have pressed the ER doctor for a little more information, but she sounded scared. I told her I'd be right there and snapped the phone closed and jammed it into the pocket of my white coat. I only wore the white coat when I needed the pockets. My usual surgical scrubs weren't equipped to hold my wallet, my cell phone, and the on-call phone.

Stupid call phone. I was supposed to be heading to the OR.

Stupid phone? Stupid you. You're not even supposed to be on call. Why don't you tell Hank to show up on time and hold his own phone? You should get your head examined . . . always covering you partner's ass.

I'd debated going to a shrink to get my head examined, but not because I kept foolishly covering the tracks of my lazy colleague, Hank. The dominant voice in my head (I called him Lou) was slowly becoming more vocal. Lou voiced thoughts I would never have. I was a nice person. Lou . . . well . . . he was a bit more blunt and crass.

Stop bad-mouthing me. I'm not the dipshit who invented a call phone. *Good-bye, pager; here's something even more intrusive. Hooray for administrators and their "instant access" plan to interrupt your day at any moment.*

But this was a real emergency—a real reason to interrupt my already busy surgical schedule. I stepped out of my office and almost plowed over my nurse, Shyla.

"Whoa," she yelped, throwing her hands up over her face in an act of self-defense. When Shyla realized she wasn't going to be crushed, she lowered them and looked up at me. She was a petite half-Indian woman who stood five feet tall with clogs on. She'd suffered more than one collision, so she was right to cower.

I was to blame for those crashes. Apparently I couldn't see things below my chest. The bruises and scars on my shins proved it. I stood six foot three without clogs and with my hair patted down. Actually, I didn't own clogs, and possessed only a few millimeters of hair.

I pointed a finger to the stairwell. "Sorry . . . ER."

Shyla chased after me down the hallway, struggling to keep up with my long strides. "Do you want me to hold the call phone until Dr. Patten shows up?"

"Yeah, thanks," I said. I slapped the phone into her hand.

"Have you thought about Peru?"

"Still thinking," I called back as I slipped into the stairwell and escaped further questioning. It was tempting to help others by going on the medical mission trip with Shyla and some of my fellow doctors, but I also needed some time to myself.

As I flew down the stairs from the surgical floor to the ER, my heart raced with the thrill of being the end of the line defense against Death. My hands felt clammy for the same reason. It's exciting to be needed, as if Gotham just lit up the Bat Signal for me. But this call to duty usually meant a visit to the ER to try to save someone standing one foot in the grave.

And the other on a banana peel.

I tried to ignore Lou as I waved my badge in front of the sensor near the back door of the ER. As soon as it clicked, I shoved it wide, too impatient for it to automatically open. I strode down the hall and a nurse looked at me with a pale face. "Room 3. Good luck."

Room 3. The Code Room. A patient in Room 3 had one of three future destinations—the ICU, the OR, or the morgue.

Vivian, the ER doc, met me in the hallway. She was a cutie, even with her hair pushed sloppily off to one side and her face a little paler than its usual Filipino tone. She must have been finishing a night shift.

She skipped past the pleasantries and dove into the patient's history. "She came in a few hours ago saying her breathing was tight. She had a thyroidectomy four days ago, but her voice was good and her neck felt soft. She's pretty fat, though. She's got a history of asthma and anxiety, so I worked on those angles, but now she's decompensating." Decompensating was the nice way of saying circling the drain.

I pushed past Vivian into Room 3. The patient's anxiety and asthma didn't matter. Vivian called because her patient was slowly suffocating. Blood from a recent neck surgery can accumulate under the skin and muscles can pinch off the airway without any obvious external signs. As a Head and Neck surgeon, I'd seen plenty of similar cases, and had cut open plenty of necks to establish an airway when all else failed.

Mrs. Childs, an overweight African-American woman, sat up in Bed 3, leaning forward with her arms stretched in front of her, grasping the shiny silver handrails like she was clutching the handlebars of a chopper. Sweat glistened on her forehead. Her disheveled gown covered her private parts, but fat legs and arms bulged out from under it in every direction as if the gown were a fist clenching down on a ball of dough. She had scars on shins, too, and she didn't even seem that tall. She barely glanced at me when I entered.

I heard a slightly wet sucking noise as she inhaled and exhaled. It was one of the worst sounds in the world, or at least my world. It meant her airway was narrow at the level of the thyroid surgery. If it wasn't blood choking her to death, it could be paralyzed vocal cords slowly swelling together. They sometimes wait a day or two after surgery before announcing their intent to kill the patient.

No time for guessing games, numbnuts. You better get her upstairs before she closes off her airway. They don't have shit down here, and as soon as she codes, it's going to be absolute fucking mayhem.

Mrs. Childs finally looked straight at me, eyes piercing. "Don't let me die." Her stern look reminded me of my basketball coach from years ago. In a tight game, he'd look straight through me and say, "Do what you were made to do." That meant dominate. Forget the coordinated offense and all the plans; just go out and put my heart into it. And for some reason, him saying that pumped me up more than any other pep talk ever could.

I locked eyes with her and felt the same burst of adrenaline. "I'll do everything I can for you." I knew better than to promise she'd be all right but I had no problem offering her my guarantee to do everything I could to keep her alive. I give that guarantee to everyone in need.

The nice thing about working in a small hospital like this one is word travels fast. Great when you need help, not so great when your partner Hank has an affair with a nurse on 4North. In this case, I needed assistance. Owen, the anesthesiologist working the ER, and one of his nurse anesthetist students had clearly gotten wind of my Room 3 airway emergency, because they ran in carrying a fiber-optic scope.

I turned to Owen's student. "Get the OR ready for an emergency tracheostomy. We'll be up in a minute."

Lou, despite all the vulgarities, was right. This ER wasn't equipped for me to do anything definitive, and I'd prefer the OR over the morgue as this patient's exit strategy. I couldn't help but take every death as a personal affront to my skills as a surgeon and my value as a human. It would be far easier for both Mrs. Childs and me if she lived.

Owen seemed to trust my judgment because he just nodded as he kicked the lever to unlock the wheels on Mrs. Childs's bed so he could pull it out of its bay. "The OR's empty, and by the time we get there they'll be ready." He gave the bed a big shove, and we headed out the door.

"Well, at least have your patient lie down," an ER nurse snarled from behind us. "Safety first." She snapped the workplace catchphrase to the satisfaction of unseen administrators.

"That's a negative." Owen flicked the words out like a snake tasting the air just before biting. I'd worked with him long enough to know he didn't tolerate being told what to do, especially when he knew he was right. Lying Mrs. Childs flat would only narrow her airway even further.

"I'm glad you're here," Owen said as we wheeled Mrs. Childs to the elevator,

"Ditto," I replied.

Our patient looked up at me. "You guys the A-Team?"

"Yep. They just don't let me wear my gold chains to work," Owen told her with a smile.

I pity the fool who makes bad Mr. T jokes.

Mrs. Childs didn't smile back as she resumed her gaspy breathing. A little drool escaped her wide-open mouth and dripped from her chin onto the bed. She made no effort to wipe away the sticky string of saliva hanging off her lip. She was in survival mode.

As we wheeled her into the room, I told Owen, "No sedation, no paralysis."

"Of course not." He smiled like he already had his own plan, and it didn't include sedation. Owen wore thin little wire glasses that matched his delicate silver hair, and his narrow face bore the creases of a wise man. His look augmented his credibility. I trusted him.

Owen sprayed a bolus of lidocaine into Mrs. Childs's right nostril to numb it up. He was still planning to scope her. "I'll take a look. Maybe we can get it this way."

Owen was one of those people who are open-minded *enough*. In other words, after he tried his own way once and failed, he was willing to let someone else try. This doesn't sound open-minded, unless you're used to working with people who fail once and then insist on failing numerous additional times, never changing their plan of attack or allowing help.

The assistants transferred Mrs. Childs onto the operating room bed and then hooked her up to all the monitors in a flash. The room was cold and sterile and full of serious-looking equipment. Completely unwelcoming, and one of my favorite places to be. I now had home-court advantage against Death.

Mrs. Childs needed an endotracheal tube to create a passage between her swelling vocal cords. The endotracheal is the "breathing tube" of general anesthesia, the sole means of delivering oxygen to someone no longer awake enough to take a breath on their own. I knew Owen would first snake a flexible fiber-optic scope through her nose, down her airway, and into her trachea, and then use the scope

5

as a guide to thread the endotracheal tube down the same path.

I gowned and gloved as a scrub nurse I didn't recognize frantically organized the sterile instruments. Then I took my position on Mrs. Childs's right side.

Owen and his nurse anesthetist were ready. He sprayed a little more lidocaine into Mrs. Child's nose, which would numb up her airway a little, but still allow her to move and breathe. He stopped and looked at the clock. "I like to give it a full five minutes to take effect," he told his assistant. "I've seen other docs rush before the airway was numb and accidentally trigger spasm by touching the sensitive tissues near the vocal cords. Sometimes a few extra seconds of patience can save a life."

His assistant nodded. She probably didn't have enough experience to do anything but agree with everything Owen said. Even behind the mask she looked wide-eyed and barely old enough to be there. But that was okay; the extra hands were welcome and between Owen and I, she'd never be in the position of having to make a decision.

Another thirty seconds dripped by. Scenarios played through my head—every possible way this could go wrong. Just being too rough with the scope in the nose could cause a nosebleed. Once blood got on the scope tip, the procedure would become a life-and-death game of Pin the Tail on the Donkey.

Owen held the scope so Mrs. Childs could see it. "I'm going to put this into your nose and your airway now. It's going to feel weird, but just keep breathing."

Mrs. Childs looked at him, bewildered, yet she still nodded. She would have agreed to anything just to be able to breathe again, I suspected.

Owen drove the three-millimeter-wide scope into Mrs. Childs's right nostril. He put the back of his left hand on her right cheek and used his index finger and thumb to gently feed the scope forward. Scopes are great tools, with flexible tips that flex and extend to turn corners. There's no better way to visualize an airway. When the scope reached the back of her nose, Owen angled it around the bend and looked down toward her vocal cords.

Mrs. Childs looked at me, searching for reassurance. "Keep breathing, nice and slowly," I told her.

"Everything is swollen, but I can see the opening," Owen said as he continued advancing the scope. Then he looked at Mrs. Childs. "Take a slow, deep breath. You'll feel your airway get pinched off for a second, but don't worry. We've got it under control."

Easier said than done.

Owen advanced the scope into the narrowest part of Mrs. Childs's airway, turning the already small opening into no opening at all. I knew he'd thread the endotracheal tube over the scope and into her airway to establish a bigger, safer air passage just a second later. But Mrs. Childs didn't give him a second. She panicked, pushing Owen back and yanking the scope out of her nose and then starting to swing her arms. Instead of following Owen's directions to breathe slowly, she tried to inhale deeply, making the loose, swollen tissue collapse into her airway. Her eyes bulged with fear as she choked herself.

I put a hand on her shoulder. "Slow breaths. *Slow.*"

She batted my hand out of the way. No way was she going to relax. She tried gasping, mouth wide, eyes wider in disbelief that her lungs weren't inflating as she expected. Her arms flailed and then her hands clutched at her neck. I reached for her one more time and she pushed me away.

"Knock her out! Get ready, Rees!" Owen grabbed Mrs. Childs in a bear hug and nodded to his nurse anesthetist to go. Her hands trembled as she switched from one syringe in the IV line to the next, pushing in one medicine after the other.

Okay, numbnuts, take a slow, deep breath and don't fuck this up. We've got this.

Mrs. Childs passed out before the drugs even began to circulate. Owen let her go, then positioned himself at the head of the bed as her pulse oximeter, the small device that monitors a patient's blood oxygen level, started to lose pitch. The lower the oxygen level, the lower the pitch. With every one of Mrs. Childs's heartbeats, the pitch sank lower into baritone.

Time to sink or swim. "This is going to hurt," I said to no one in particular as I stepped in to do my part.

But not as much as dying.

Mrs. Childs let out a giant fart. Bodies do this when they're trying to die—sphincter control is one of the first things to go.

I pushed our patient's chin up with the back of my left hand to expose her neck. "Hold her," I told Owen, and he grabbed her chin and pulled.

In a normal situation, a nurse would sterilely prep the field. But that takes time. Mrs. Childs didn't have time.

"Fifteen." I held out my hand for the 15 blade, the smaller of my scalpel options. My fingers tingled as I wrapped them around the knife the scrub tech handed me. I looked down, expecting to see the scalpel trembling.

Want me to do it?

NO.

Never give the voices control. That's how you get diagnosed with schizophrenia.

Oh, puh-lease.

Lou *is* short for lunatic.

Fine, fine. You do it. But take your time. She can hold her breath a minute. Everyone can go two minutes without air. Skin divers go underwater that long, and they're swimming, for Chrissake.

Despite sweating like one, Mrs. Childs wasn't an athlete, and two minutes feels like an eternity to an impatient surgeon. But it wouldn't take two minutes to get her an airway.

I looked at my hand again. The blade was still. I turned my attention to the row of sutures linked across the front of Mrs. Child's neck like stitches on a baseball. No sense in trying to cut them out one by one. Instead, I pushed the knife into the far end of the line and watched the wound unzip as I pulled across the suture line.

Each deep suture released a palpable pop as the blade broke it. The thin layer of neck muscles under the fat popped into view, sutured from top to bottom. I pushed the knife in at the top suture, felt its tip hit the thyroid cartilage, pulled back a bit, and swept down. The middle of the neck is a safe area to be aggressive—no big nerves or blood vessels, and in this case, no thyroid. Nothing but skin, fat, and muscles before the cartilage of the trachea.

When I sliced the muscle layer apart, a cupful of white, milky liquid gushed out. It looked fake, like cheesy horror movie fake. I imagined the groans of a movie theater audience.

White? Where's the blood?

"What the fuck?" Owen muttered from the head of the table.

Ditto.

I didn't take time to answer either of them. My first thought was that Mrs. Childs's neck was filled with the dinner she'd eaten last night. Maybe my partner had accidentally cut a small hole in her esophagus during her surgery four days earlier. Bizarre.

With my left hand, I grabbed her trachea through the fluid and slid my index finger down its front wall until I felt the cricoid, the cartilage ring below the Adam's apple. It's the only complete cartilage ring of the trachea, so it doesn't compress when pushed. I slid farther down and over the next cartilage ring, and then one more: the right spot for a tracheostomy.

The nurse suctioned the milky fluid away so I could see my fingertip on our patient's airway. I cut an upside down *U* shape into the front of it.

"Pickups and tube," I called as I handed the knife back. I grabbed the pickups, or tweezers, in my left hand, and the endotracheal tube in my right.

I flipped the flap of trachea I'd just cut upward with the pickups. This opened a view straight into the airway. The lining looked normal: pink, smooth, glistening with a thin layer of mucus, and not at all swollen.

I threaded the end of the tube into Mrs. Childs's trachea and held it in place with my left hand. Owen handed me the connection from his machine, and I hooked it up to the tube. The anesthetist squeezed the bag at the other end, forcing 100-percent oxygen into our patient's lungs.

Everything was good.

I sighed, the tension running out of my muscles like a balloon deflating. My posture loosened.

Don't pee yourself with excitement, numbnuts; you were just doing what you were supposed to do. It's not like you sank a game-winning three from half-court. This was a slam dunk. Her airway was right there.

"Nice job," Owen said. "Hope nothing like this happens down in Peru. You're coming, right?"

Owen was soon leaving for a medical mission to Peru. Shyla was part of his small team, and she'd been asking—more like politely pestering—me to join them.

I'd timed my own vacation for the same week as Shyla's medical mission because I hated working without her, but I preferred vacationing alone. I got enough of humans all week long. Leaving them behind calmed me, and, more importantly, Lou.

I had to admit Shyla's polite pestering was making me think twice, though. Using my vacation time to help someone other than myself was probably the ultimate way to give back. Part of me felt like helping people would settle a debt; a payback of sorts for all the help I'd received throughout my own schooling and training. A karmic balance. But I couldn't think of all the anonymous people I might help in Peru when I still had an actual patient in front of me waiting to be treated.

Once Mrs. Childs's oxygen level returned to normal, I cleaned out the surgical field. There were still milky puddles in crevices, and dark, glistening clots of old blood from the original surgery. When I irrigated the wound with saline, a shimmery layer of fat accumulated on the surface of the water, resembling a greasy soup. The milk wasn't from the esophagus; it was lymph fluid. Mrs. Childs had a lymph leak that had accumulated in the thyroid space.

Could that lymph fluid trigger swelling or compression of the airway? Guess so. Too bad no one would give me the answer, though. I would've been perfectly content having all the answers to the universe, even if no one believed me. The Cassandra Curse didn't sound like a curse at all.

I looked for any potential lymph leaks. Then I put a few silk ties, or individual sutures, around some fatty areas at the lower aspect of the surgical field because the lymph channels run through fat.

Next I converted the makeshift airway to a proper tracheostomy. Soon a rigid, curved plastic tube was in place, one end in the trachea and the other sticking straight out from the neck wound. I closed the remainder of the wound on the sides of the "trach" tube layer by layer, leaving the central part loose. If more lymph fluid accumulated, it would leak out of Mrs. Childs's neck near the trach tube. Hope for the best, prepare for the worst.

I looked at Owen and shook my head. This was a crazy victory. Not quite a Hail Mary, but definitely a scramble as time ran off the clock. Surgeons don't fist-pump to celebrate victory; we respond more like soldiers in the trenches while shells fly overhead. I could imagine the conversation Owen and I were having in our thoughts. *That was a close one. Yeah, I think it just shaved a year off my life. Any closer and...*

I took a slow, deep breath and exhaled. I still had a whole day of operating ahead of me and was already an hour behind. Time to get back to my regular schedule now that Mrs. Childs was stable.

My first case was a relaxing set of ear tubes. Owen held a mask over a three-year-old girl's mouth to deliver an inhalational anesthetic. She tried to scream in defiance, but the deep breath she took to fill her lungs sucked in so much anesthetic that by the time she was ready to scream, all she could muster was a whimper. Her fingers twitched as if typing a message on an invisible keyboard and then fell still as she succumbed to the gas-induced slumber.

Owen adjusted the mask over her face. "Shyla says you have a *solo* camping trip planned. Sounds pretty easy to cancel and go to Peru for some mission work instead." His voice had just enough inflection to hint there was some hope in the question.

I pulled the microscope up to the girl's ear and took a seat on a stool. Inserting tubes sounds like something aliens do, but it simply means putting tubes into the eardrums to remove the fluid retained behind them. It's the most common surgical procedure in the United

States.

"You should call it a surgical mission. Mission work sounds less exciting," I said.

"It's not real work. And these people need a surgeon. You're not good for anything else, so you might as well spend your days doing what you were built for." Owen's surgical mask hid his grin, but I knew it was there. "It's kind of true about you types," he chuckled.

He's right. Surgery is a dead-end job. It's not like you're qualified to do anything else.

I'd been considering Peru, it was true, but not quite committing to it. I needed some time away from this all-consuming career, where I spent all day jumping through hoops without time to relax or even go on a date. Leaving the hectic Bay Area for a trip in the Sierras would clear my head, maybe even of Lou. Going on a medical mission with people I didn't know well was full of risk—the risk of having a crappy vacation.

C'mon, dude. Live a little.

Owen seemed to sense my hesitation. "Ziggler's coming. You know Ziggler?"

I knew Ziggler—a general surgeon who appeared to have life dragging his slumped body from one place to another by an invisible tether while he frowned in disapproval. There must be something more to him if Owen thought his presence made the trip more enticing.

I shrugged. "I've met him. But you know I'm not fluent in Spanish, right?"

Owen's hidden grin seemed to grow. "Shyla will interpret."

"Peru has nasty parasites," I said. "I don't want to end up looking like a leper."

Owen shook his head. "I'm asking you to perform surgery, not sleep with prostitutes. You're not going to get any parasites. We've got sprays and netting and drugs. We're invincible." He clapped his chest twice and pointed at me, like he was motivating a quarterback rather than a doctor afraid of losing a liver to larval infestation.

Although I was even more curious about the mission, I needed to take a few minutes to finish the procedure in front of me. I tend to not talk much while operating. If it were up to me, everyone in the world would be a ninja, with silent focus and cutting efficiency for all life's missions. Even the easy ones.

But my need to concentrate didn't stop Owen from talking as he stood at the head of the operative table, one hand holding the mask over our young patient's face. "Peru's great. We're going to a remote town in a jungle valley that joins the Andes to the Amazon. It's unbelievably beautiful. You'd even have some time for some solo hikes in the jungle . . . if that's what you single guys are into these days."

He said it like I was one of those weirdoes who runs off into the wilderness because he can't fit into the "rigors" of society, such as maintaining a job or showering regularly. Just because I was single didn't mean I was shunning the universe to go hide under a tree stump.

You're pretty fuckin' weird. You won't let anyone touch your feet.

I pushed on the patient's temple as a subtle suggestion for Owen to reposition her. He grasped the top of her head with his free hand and turned her face away from me, putting her ear in front of the microscope.

I made a slit in the eardrum with a tiny knife. Boogery fluid oozed out the incision. I vacuumed it out with a tiny suction catheter, which made absurd sounds like trying to suck the last bit of milkshake out of a glass with a straw. A minute later, the tube was in. The whole process was over before the patient's parents had even started to calm down. I knew they were somewhere out there in the waiting room, crawling back and forth across the ceiling, scared to death about what might happen to their child. Nothing provokes more anxiety than a child needing medical attention, and probably nothing else should.

While we waited for our patient to awaken from the gas, the nurse waved a big white wand over her. The other end of the wand was attached to a device that looked like a DVD player, only without a tray for the disc.

She noticed my confused look. "We have to wand every patient to ensure there aren't any retained sponges," she explained. "Every case requires documentation."

Each surgical sponge or piece of gauze has a radio frequency thread woven into it to make it detectable. Patients have died from surgeons leaving sponges in the abdomen, so I understood the need to wand in many cases, but not this one. "A sponge or gauze wouldn't even fit in her ear canal," I protested.

She continued the wanding. "Sorry, rules are rules."

I kept my mouth shut and let loose a heavy sigh out my nose.

Owen snapped his fingers. "No wands in Peru," he sang.

Probably no arbitrary, moronic rules in Peru, either.

Ten minutes later, the arbitrary rulemakers were back at it in the pre-op holding area. As I finished the paperwork to prepare my next patient for surgery, a woman in a business suit approached. Her red name badge announced she was a peri-operative administrator. And the tight look on her face, matched by an equally stiff posture, meant she thought she was important.

"Dr. Rees Baker?" She glanced down at my badge to confirm my name. But I wasn't wearing it, just a generic one that simply read DOCTOR.

A week earlier, the badge had magically appeared on my desk. When I'd asked my partner about it, he said the staff wanted to better differentiate roles in health care situations. Nurses got badges reading NURSE in big letters, and doctors DOCTOR. We were supposed to wear them along with our name badges so patients could easily identify both the person helping them as well as their job title. I'd started wearing just the generic badge to mock the depersonalization infiltrating our healthcare system.

"That's me," I answered.

The administrator hesitated and took a longer look at my badge. Her face twisted into a scowl but she didn't comment on it. "We're auditing preoperative orders and paperwork in preparation for the upcoming inspection. We noticed you didn't order a pregnancy test for your next patient."

I looked down at the paperwork I was trying to finish. "Because she has no chance of being pregnant."

The administrator pursed her lips and even rolled her eyes a little. "Surely, Dr. Baker, you know better than to believe a woman when she says that."

I'd believe you weren't pregnant, you ugly toad.

I shared Lou's hatred of smarmy attitudes. Good thing I had a built-in Lou filter to keep from speaking his words out loud, though. "My patient can't be pregnant. She doesn't have a uterus."

The administrator straightened like she'd just been goosed. "What, what, what?" she muttered to herself as she flipped through the papers on her clipboard. Then she flipped through them a second time as she walked to my patient's bed, high heels clacking against the floor the whole way. She looked at the patient and the identification sticker on the chart at the foot of the bed, and then again, before clacking back to me. "There's no documentation of a hysterectomy in Nancy Morgan's surgical history. The rule is, without documentation, we need a pregnancy test."

I smiled. "Nope."

She didn't smile back. "Dr. Baker, this is not a time for games. And it isn't your choice. Nancy Morgan needs a pregnancy test. It is one of the eight preoperative imperatives." The administrator's voice raised in octave and volume. "She is of the childbearing age."

I almost giggled. The word "childbearing" gets me every time. It's the idea of a "child bear." Imagine a woman giving birth to a bear cub, a cute one, like Winnie the Pooh. Most women have babies, some have child bears.

"This isn't a joke, Dr. Baker," the administrator snapped, obviously not sharing my cuddly mental image.

"As I said before, my patient doesn't have a uterus and she didn't have a hysterectomy." I kept my voice low to protect the confidentiality of this information; the pre-op holding area was just a row of beds separated by thin curtains. "Nancy Morgan is a man— *was* a man—before the operation."

Most people, when confronted with the truth, will admit error.

But some, like this nameless administrator, like to proceed as if the facts are irrelevant. I was facing a bulldozer.

The Bulldozer merely hardened her face and continued to plow ahead. "That might be true. But Mrs. Morgan chose 'female' for gender on her admission paperwork. That means she needs a pregnancy test."

I looked The Bulldozer directly in the eyes with the hope I could beam a few brain cells over to her. "*Mrs.* Morgan has an X and Y chromosome. Her gender identity might be in flux, her external anatomy might be redesigned, but I assure you, no one has installed a functional uterus into her."

"I'm sorry, but rules are rules. We are mandated to check every woman for pregnancy prior to receiving any anesthetic."

Sorry, rules are rules. There must have been some sort of administrative brainwashing to replace thinking with that boneheaded mantra.

"I'm not writing that order," I said in defense of the ability to think rationally.

"Then you are not in compliance. That's not allowed." The Bulldozer slammed a high heel down and spun away, her footsteps pellet-gunning across the floor back to my patient.

Owen stepped up behind me. "Revenge of the C students," he whispered in my ear.

I turned toward him. "C students?"

Owen chuckled. "All the morons who could hardly finish high school get desk jobs here at the hospital. And while you were at medical school and residency, they got promoted up the chain. Now those same buffoons are running the place. The people not smart enough to get into medical school are your boss."

"Yours too," I muttered.

As The Bulldozer tried to explain the need for a pregnancy test to Mrs. Morgan, my patient sat up in bed. Setting aside her usual feminine voice for her former bass, she looked straight at the administrator. "Are you trying to embarrass me, or are you that fucking stupid?"

When The Bulldozer's face lit up like a taillight, I felt a bit jealous. I'd been wishing I could turn off my Lou-filter, but maybe I didn't need to. Mrs. Morgan was doing the job just fine on her own.

The Bulldozer turned and clacked her way out of the holding area without so much as glancing at me. People like her with their blind devotion to rules and algorithms are killing the joy of medicine for those of us who like to think.

Owen laughed. "And *that* is why you need to join me on a medical mission. Not a single bureaucrat. Just real medicine." He patted me on the back of the shoulder and walked away.

"I'll go," I said. The words leapt out of my throat like one of those unexpected burps that shocks you as much as everyone around you. It must have been Lou. Maybe my filter wasn't as good as I thought.

Owen stopped and looked back. "Really?"

I nodded. "I could use a dose of what real medicine's supposed to be like."

Even if I had to go to Peru to find it.

Chapter 2

A week later I found myself rushing to the airport to catch my flight to Peru. I'd forgotten about that rule of being at the airport three hours early for an international flight until Owen called me on his way to the airport. Sorry, rules are rules.

When I caught up to the group at our departure gate, I was surprised to see Shyla talking to a slightly familiar woman in sunglasses, which the brightness of the overhead lights did not seem to warrant. Indoor sunglasses meant Los Angeles to me. Yuck.

Ziggler, the fourth member of our team, stood just past Shyla reading a throwaway medical journal. I assumed he was using it as a sleep aid for the flight. Ziggler looked like a giant next to Shyla. He was almost my height, but easily had fifty pounds on me. His hair was graying and he was probably around fifty, a little younger and not as silver as Owen. He looked like half the men in the airport – chubby, white, and middle-aged.

I walked up to Shyla. "Hey," I started, but the woman in sunglasses turned toward me.

"Oh, please, can't you see we're having a private conversation?"

Her voice made it clear she considered me an intruder, and that's when I recognized her. Famous internet celebrity "Crazy" Kat Kentfield, Shyla's younger, taller sister. They both looked like they were still in their twenties instead of their thirties and shared many of the same features, including full smooth cheeks differentiated only by the dimple on the left side of Kat's face.

It's a scar, not a dimple, Lou corrected, but it didn't make a difference. Shyla was very attractive, but her sister was stunning, even with a scar.

I was surprised to see Kat, not because I get weak in the knees at the sight of cute celebrities, but because I knew from Shyla that she lived in Los Angeles (I was right about the indoor sunglasses). Kat had been one of the early YouTube sensations, somehow turning an endearing song and video into a whole album. She then rolled with her fame for years by releasing a song here and there and doing ridiculous things like wearing a dress made of lettuce to stay in the limelight. Shyla made it a point not to talk about Kat at work, but telling me her sister was coming along on the medical mission would have been worth mentioning.

Owen didn't say shit about her coming, either. Does she even have any medical knowledge?

Kat's lipstick-caked lips twisted in an ugly sneer. "Do you want a photo, or are you just going to stand there and stare?"

Shyla hardly wore any makeup, and her face didn't seem capable of snarling. Perhaps the sisters' resemblance ended at their physical similarities. I turned my gaze from Kat to Shyla. "Are those my only two options?"

Shyla grinned. "This is my *charming* sister, Kat."

Kat's scowl dropped and her posture relaxed. She even blushed a little through her brown skin.

I extended my hand toward Kat. "Hi, I'm Rees." She took it meekly, and we shook. Nice to see a little humility still remained in the celebrity brat.

Celebrity brat. Celebratty. How had the entertainment industry not already come up with that mash-up? Brangelina. Bromance. Why not celebratty, too?

Kat withdrew her hand from mine. "Sorry, I'm having a rough day. I thought you were another stalker type," she said. She regaled us with stories of the cab driver who'd offered to waive his fare if he could take a selfie of her kissing him on the cheek and the security guy joking he'd like to give her a full-body search.

I apologized on behalf of groper and stalker types everywhere, though mostly I was sorry I'd been so easily mistaken for one. I wasn't even slack-jawed and drooling.

Shyla smiled at me with doe eyes. "Kat decided to join us! It'll be a great help to have an extra set of hands." The look on Shyla's face asked me to spare her from my numerous questions, so I just nodded.

Kat nodded, too. "It's been a rough week, and I could use the escape. I've always had an interest in medicine."

I struggled to concentrate on what Kat was saying, distracted by the skinny young guy behind her who wouldn't stop staring. No wonder she'd snapped at me. The guy wasn't even looking my way and I still found him unnerving.

As soon as Kat's radar picked him up, she turned, stuck out her tongue, and waved her arms in the air. She made a "blah-blah-blah-blah" sound and then wagged her tongue back and forth at him. Then, as quickly as she started, she stopped. The man didn't even flinch; he just kept staring. When he pulled out his phone, she turned away before he could snap a picture.

The gate agent announced pre-boarding for the disabled and those who had ritualistically sacrificed a child for the honor of getting on the plane first, and a crowd of passengers began moving forward in anticipation of boarding.

Owen was leaning against a wall talking on his cell phone, obviously not concerned about claiming his spot. I left the line and walked over just in time to hear him say "good-bye," followed by "I love you, too," to his wife before hanging up.

"Why isn't your wife coming?" I asked.

Owen put his phone in his pocket. "She came once. Shyla's husband, too. But nonmedical people don't get it, and it's a lot to ask people to spend their vacation doing menial medical tasks."

"What about Shyla's sister?"

Owen shrugged. "Kat might make things interesting. Every trip always has a surprise. She might be it, but something tells me we shouldn't expect too much from her."

I smiled. "As long as she isn't a bureaucrat. You guaranteed me a trip without them, remember."

Owen laughed heartily and slapped me on the back. Then he nonchalantly cut in line until he was right behind Shyla, Kat, and Ziggler. He seemed to somehow glide right through the crowd, whereas I had to excuse myself as I bumped into people and collected nasty looks while trying to keep up. The staring fanboy gave me a glare, probably for interrupting his gazing at Kat.

When I scanned my ticket at the agent's kiosk, the machine made a loud beep. The agent grabbed my boarding pass and told me I had a new seat. They'd probably found the two smelliest people on the

20

plane and sandwiched me in between them.

When I boarded, I found I'd been moved to the front row of economy. Owen and Ziggler were next to each other in the row behind me.

I turned back to look at Owen. "Don't tell me you paid that hundred-dollar ransom to buy us seats with an extra quarter-inch of legroom."

Owen shook his head. "Shyla just told me Kat did it, when she upgraded the two of them into business class."

I didn't know if Kat had paid a fee, or somehow gotten it waived thanks to her celebrity status, but I didn't care.

Who knows, maybe she gave the ticket agent a kiss.

Next to Owen, Ziggler made a face. "Business class? How's she going to make it in a jeep for six hours in the sticky jungle air?"

I twisted more so I could look at Owen straight in the face. "You didn't say anything about a six-hour jungle jeep ride."

Owen grinned. "Hmm, I'm surprised I skipped that. It *is* a major selling point. And if it were only six hours, that would be even better."

I laughed. "You think the airline would mind me ripping off my seat cushion so I could bring it along for extra padding? Or maybe we can get Shyla to snatch us some pillows from business class."

Moments later, two young men with matching hipster beards sat in the seats next to me, both wearing the faint smell of alcohol. It was either a buzz left over from a night that had never ended, or the duo had decided it was never too early to start celebrating their trip to Peru.

Once we were in the air, I kept my eyes closed as much as possible in a vain attempt to get some sleep.

Beard Number Two came back from the bathroom. "You know who I just standing in the aisle? Kat Kentfield," he said to Beard Number One sitting next to me.

"Crazy Kat? She's messed up. She pissed her pants at the Grammys," Beard One whispered.

"I'd still do her," Beard Two said a bit too loudly, unable to maintain a whisper. "Did you see those leaked photos? The topless Valentine one is hot."

"Oh yeah, don't get me wrong, she's smokin'," Beard One said under his breath. "I'd fuck the shit out of her if I had the chance . . . but she's got issues."

Hey, buddy. Why don't you open an eyelid just far enough to give them the stink eye? C'mon, do it for me.

I thought you would have liked that sort of foul talk.

Hey, you're going to a faraway place with a beautiful woman. I'm rooting for you. But I like to keep the linen clean as much as you do. That just sounds . . . messy.

Oh, all right.

I opened my eyes to see a blonde flight attendant in the aisle in front of us. I braced myself for her to berate Beards One and Two, but instead she turned to me. "Dr. Baker?"

"Yes?" I answered. Both Beards looked at me.

"Kat Kentfield said she's sorry about the mix-up earlier and would like to offer you a make-up mimosa." The flight attendant beamed as she held a champagne flute toward me. Her eyes begged for the story, but I wasn't about to confess Kat had mistaken me for a stalker.

"How sweet of her," I said, and took the drink as my grizzly neighbors gawked. I turned and raised the glass to them, turning the corner of my mouth up just a tiny bit as I gave them a nod.

And then I drank, closing my eyes and letting Lou have the fun of imagining their looks of amazement and envy.

Chapter 3

I woke—empty champagne flute either collected by the flight attendant or stolen by one of the Beards as a Kat souvenir—as we descended into Lima. Traveling to South America on an overnight flight is the way to go, and only a two-hour time change means no jet lag.

You get excited about the lamest shit.

I wished we had time to explore Lima itself, but instead we shuffled to the domestic flights terminal. The yellow tiled floor and painted white concrete pillars reminded me of just about every outdated airport I'd ever set foot in. And even though there was plenty of Spanish on the signage, there was also English. I felt more like I was in Los Angeles County a few hours south of my home than in South America.

Soon enough, we were on a much smaller plane to Tarapoto, complete with a crew giving instructions in Spanish, noisy propellers, and plenty of nauseating turbulence. The aircraft was so ancient it still had ashtrays in the armrests. *Now* I felt like I was somewhere foreign.

The town of Tarapoto sits high in the Andes in the northern part of Peru. It's a tourist hub of sorts, only without looking like one. From there, tourists take trips into the cloud forest or venture down into the Amazon for hiking or whitewater rafting.

When we left the airport and got to our hotel, Owen gathered us into a group. "This is it, your last bit of civilization for the next eight days. Time to load up on junk food and booze. No need to change much money; there's nowhere to spend it once we leave here."

Shyla took Owen's recommendation to stock up seriously, and she and Kat retreated to their hotel room to examine Kat's bags for forgotten necessities. Ziggler and Owen, on the other hand, were ready to head out to buy liquor.

I suspected the day would dissolve slowly and painfully in front of my eyes if I waited for Shyla. Having no desire to stock up on alcohol, I ventured out on my own, equipped with a pretty good sense of direction and a rudimentary understanding of Spanish. I was fine going solo, considering I would have been alone backpacking in the Sierras if I hadn't decided to go along on the medical mission.

Walking alone, even in a town, is relaxing. No distractions. No opinions. Best of all, no bureaucrats.

A bustling marketplace congested the streets in the town center. Wood tables and carts jam-packed with brightly colored fruits and vegetables filled the area under a large shade structure. Old-fashioned steel hanging scales poked up everywhere. I could buy spiny yellow fruits I'd never seen before by the pound . . . or was it kilogram? Was Peru metric? I couldn't remember.

The pavilion itself consisted of a wooden beam skeleton with corrugated steel roofing. This was the original warehouse store. I wove through its narrow aisles, squeezing my way between the locals, just taking it all in, except for the raw meat aisle. Even in the produce section, the scent of raw animal flesh and blood found its way between the strong citrus odors, triggering a twinge of nausea that forced me to pick up something fruity to sniff instead. A surgeon who doesn't like the smell of raw flesh sounds almost like an oxymoron, but in the OR, things rarely smell, except the electrocautery—which smells like burning meat. Human meat.

One of the stands had little plastic bottles labeled SANGRE DE DRAGO. I knew enough medical Spanish to know "sangre" meant "blood." Blood of the Dragon?

I looked at the bottles but hesitated to pick one up. The stand's owner watched me with a wide smile. She wore a black bowler like Charlie Chaplin's. The tiny hat was clearly a few sizes too small, and it was almost floating off the top of her head, just like a Chaplin gag.

"Do you speak English?" I asked.

The woman smiled, which might have meant *yes*. I would have been more likely to believe her if she'd actually said, "Yes," though. I'd seen too many non-English-speaking patients back home who'd smiled and nodded . . . to every single question I asked.

"Sangre de Drago? Dragon's Blood?" I asked.

"Sí," the woman said.

Yep, no English.

The woman drew a slow breath and found the words. "The sap of the tree is red, like blood. It heals wounds and prevents infection."

My mistake. Sí, Inglés.

I'd heard of using pinesap over wounds because it would create a protective layer and had antimicrobial properties. This sort of tree must be similar. I'm convinced nature holds the answer to many of our medical questions. One of our best anti-rejection drugs for organ transplants is derived from a Japanese fungus, and that's just the beginning.

The woman opened the bottle and squeezed a drop of viscous red liquid onto her fingertip. "Just cover the wound. Better than a bandage." She squeezed her fingers together to make a thin layer across her skin.

I thanked her for the information but didn't buy a bottle. I'd stick with sutures and bandages. But I did make a mental note to search for Dragon's Blood on the Internet. I loved random medical trivia. I'd read books and even taken a course on wilderness medicine, but those had been geared toward my own backwoods adventures in the United States, not South America.

A little while later, I stumbled upon Owen and Ziggler sitting outside a small café. Owen was enjoying a rice dish, and Ziggler was pushing his food around on his plate like he was strip-mining for the last good bite but coming up empty-handed.

Owen waved me over. "Come join me and my sheep-hearted friend."

I wasn't sure what that meant, but Ziggler scowled. He shoved his fork into the yellowy rice on his plate and held a scoop up to me. "Want some *juane*?"

"I don't know, do I wan-ay?" I asked.

Ziggler ignored my joke and answered, "It's rice, olives, eggs, chicken, and rice."

"And two scoops of getting used to not having a choice of what you're going to eat for the next week," Owen said with a giggle.

I think I wan-ay puke.

I wrinkled my nose. Who knew olives were part of Peruvian

cuisine?

"Yeah, the olive and egg combo didn't do it," Ziggler grunted, letting his fork drop onto the plate.

"Take a seat," Owen said, pointing to the empty chair across from him. "Try this. It's *lomo*. You'll love it—marinated grilled sirloin with rice and French fries all mixed together to look like a salad, just for people who want to die of a heart attack. It's great." Owen stacked up a bite on his fork and held it out for me.

I waved off the fork, because eating off 1) someone else's plate in a 2) street-side, 3) third-world restaurant was just too many strikes. Let's just say my Achilles' heel is my stomach. But the food looked good and there weren't any other tourists, a sign they'd found something authentic.

Ziggler picked up his fork to give the juane one more at-bat. "I think letting Kat come along is a recipe for disaster. She represents everything wrong in America, and now we're bringing her with us? I say leave her here. We can get her on the way back." He shoved a forkful of rice into his mouth as if he were angry at the food.

Ziggler had a point. Kat epitomized American culture gone wrong. The glorification of idiots who do absurd things had gone too far. What happened to the days when pants-wetting or leaked nudie pics were a huge embarrassment?

Owen took a slow breath. "I think it's a great opportunity for her. The girl's had problems; maybe a break from the scene will help. And she gets to be with Shyla. What better person to help ground her?"

Ziggler grunted again. "She's an unknown. A lot of those people do drugs. You think she was clean and sober when she pissed her pants at the Grammys?"

"Don't worry. I'm keeping all the drugs locked up," Owen said.

Ziggler pointed his fork at me. "Did you know about this?"

He had a sort of square-jawed sternness that made me shrink back in my seat like I was a kid getting questioned by my dad about a broken window. "I'm just as surprised as you are. Shyla didn't say a word."

"Find out what you can," Ziggler said. "We need to know what we're dealing with. We go on these trips to escape the PITAs. Last thing I want is to import one."

"PITAs?" I asked.

"Pain in the ass," Owen said.

For the rest of the evening, all I could think about was how upset Shyla would be if she'd overheard our conversation. The last thing she'd ever want to do was inconvenience someone...even Ziggler.

Maybe Kat won't be a PITA. Plenty of non-medical people go on medical missions to help out. Maybe we should both give her a chance.

Or maybe not.

Chapter 4

The next morning Ziggler, Owen, and I met outside the hotel five minutes before seven a.m. We were trained to start every day on time. I guessed Shyla would have been there, too, if it weren't for Kat.

A couple minutes later, an old army truck following a slightly newer jeep rumbled up to the front of the hotel. A thick layer of brown dust blanketed both vehicles.

A slender Peruvian woman with a flowing mane of straight black hair hopped out of the back of the truck. Her jeans and T-shirt made her look more American than the locals, but her milk chocolate skin and dark eyes were clearly Peruvian.

As she approached, Owen glanced back to the hotel. Still no sign of Kat or Shyla. Ziggler mumbled something about leaving the morphine and Kat behind.

Owen said hello to the woman in Spanish, but she responded in English. Owen cleared his throat and said, "Gentlemen, meet Mila. She's our transportation."

We shared hellos. Mila's youthful face led me to guess she couldn't be more than twenty-five years old. She seemed a little taller than the other local women we'd seen, and her thin eyebrows angled upward. She looked happy.

Of course she's happy. She gets to charge gringo rates for this trip.

After we loaded our gear into the back of the truck, Owen offered me and Ziggler the jeep's front passenger seat. "It's the best ride, most comfortable seat, and best views. The only downside is the sun, but the road will be in the shade once we're in the jungle."

Before I could say anything, Ziggler piped up. "I'll take it." He glanced at the hotel. "If those girls don't get down here soon, we won't be leaving at all."

Owen looked again at the lobby of the hotel. No one.

"Let's just go," Ziggler said.

Owen didn't acknowledge him as he turned to me. "You mind rapping on their door? It's room 206."

I'd barely started back inside when I heard a voice call, "Hey, guys!" and turned to see Kat and Shyla strolling up the street carrying greasy white bags.

Kat offered me her bag. "Do you want an empanada? This one's steak."

"Thanks," I said as I took the bag.

"You're welcome," Kat replied. "You ready to go?"

Are you kidding? We've been waiting ten minutes for your late ass.

I forced a smile. "I have hot meat inside a pie crust. I'm ready to take on the world."

Owen looked at me and shrugged. Kat and Shyla were a few minutes late, but they'd brought everyone breakfast. His shrug meant it was a wash.

Ziggler licked his fingers clean after finishing his first empanada and then asked for another. Breakfast delivery apparently offset his opinion of Kat being "everything wrong in America."

You're being too harsh, buddy. She's just trying to win you guys over. This is vacation, not a neurosurgical emergency. A few minutes late is no big deal. Give her a chance.

Ziggler and Owen got into the jeep while Shyla, Kat, Mila, and I piled into the back of the truck. It was the kind of truck seen in Vietnam War movies, with a covered back lined in cushioned benches. There was far more cargo back there than just our luggage and the medical supplies we'd brought, so I figured Mila was probably doing a supply run, too.

As soon as we settled in, Mila looked at us. "I'm from Urycu. It's very remote. How did you decide to go there?"

Shyla leaned forward. "Owen went there years ago on a mission. He thought it'd be great to go back."

Mila nodded. "Most people don't go there." The way she said it sounded more like people stayed *away* from there. Maybe that was what she'd meant to say, but in her limited English just didn't know how.

Shyla beamed. "That's why we're going. To help people who never get help."

Mila smiled in approval. "I know the people will be very happy for your help."

As we headed down the mountain away from Tarapoto, excitement and anticipation crept into me. Our adventure into another world was beginning. I assumed Mila's English proficiency meant the rest of the townspeople would speak it well, too. Regardless, learning a little Spanish wouldn't hurt me. I pulled out my phrase book and started to study. The little book had helped me through a trip to Costa Rica a few years back, but that was just tourism, no medicine.

As we drove into the jungle, the air turned thick and syrupy. A layer of moisture and sweat saturated my skin, erasing all evidence of my morning shower. A slight flutter of motion sickness tickled its way across my abdomen. I shouldn't have tried to read. Or was it the empanadas upsetting my stomach?

I folded back the flap of cloth at the front of the truck bed and poked my face through the aperture, which gave me an unobstructed view just above the truck's cab. I welcomed the light breeze, the chance to glimpse the jeep ahead of us, and the road curving through the trees.

A few hours later, the paved road gave way to dirt and rocks. Our driver wove back and forth across the road as he dodged the deepest potholes, and my nausea returned. I didn't normally get carsick, but soon my sweat began to chill me despite the heat, and an acidic taste crept up my throat onto the back of my tongue.

Mila, Shyla, and Kat sat on the bench across from me, huddled together as Shyla tested her Spanish and Mila her English on each another. They noticed me looking at them and went right back to talking and giggling. I imagined they were joking about me turning from *blanco* to *verde*, maybe even placing bets as to how soon I would puke.

I leaned back to stretch, which put my stomach farther from my mouth. This was a good thing as my stomach slowly squirmed upward, looking for an escape route. I should've claimed that seat in the jeep before Ziggler.

I spotted Kat popping a pill. Had Ziggler been right about her and drugs? When Kat saw me looking, she pulled a prescription bottle out of her bag and handed it to me. Ondansetron. The best medicine for nausea, and in no way a party pill.

I shook my head. "Thanks, but not quite yet."

Yeah, numbnuts, you look so tough in front of these ladies, picking a fight with nausea and trying to win without help.

I didn't acknowledge Lou. Instead, I handed the bottle back to Kat. The idea of putting anything in my mouth, even medicine, was revolting.

When she bent forward to put the bottle away in her backpack. I spied a scopolamine patch behind her right ear. She must get carsick easily.

The neck of her shirt fell open as she repositioned her backpack. I couldn't help but look; it's a side effect of testosterone. When Kat glanced up as if she could feel my eyes resting on the top edge of her lacy pink bra, my face flushed. What color do you get when you mix green and red?

I turned back toward the flap in the canvas. The breeze helped wash away the embarrassment. I even started to feel a little better.

Maybe looking down a woman's shirt like a teenage boy cured your queasies. Perhaps this warrants further study? You're going to have to apply for a grant when you get back.

The effect lasted only a few minutes. On top of the nausea, the dirt kicked up by the jeep ahead of us was sticking to my face. I realized I'd forgotten to pack that modern travel essential: baby wipes.

"Rees," Shyla called. When I turned, she snapped a picture of me with her phone. She grinned as she looked at the screen and then turned the phone toward me. I looked like a dirty zombie. Mostly pale, with a giant stripe dirt running down the middle of my face. Very nice.

Eventually we turned off the dirt road onto an even smaller path. It wasn't more than two tire ruts cutting through the jungle, with thick vegetation trying to grow on the hump between the parallel dirt tracks. There wasn't room for any oncoming traffic.

The jungle kept getting hotter and thicker. Both vehicles slowed to navigate the road, and without the breeze, the back of our military truck heated up. Yet another reason never to join the armed forces.

At another fork in the road, we took the more overgrown path. The truck grumbled and struggled as it climbed a steep hill. My nausea abated just a little as we slowed, but when the truck hit a big pothole, a burning bolus of breakfast streaked up my esophagus like a volcano erupting. I swallowed the nasty acid back down.

The vehicles stopped abruptly, and our driver shifted the truck into park. I peeked through the flap and saw an elderly woman standing in the middle of the road in front of the jeep. I seized the opportunity to hop out of my seat, work my way to the back of the truck, and crawl over the tailgate.

Kat moved over to peek through the hole in the flap where I'd been sitting as Shyla frowned. "What's going on?" she called after me.

I held up a finger. "Just a minute," I called back. I ran to the edge of the jungle to let loose my empanadas. Of course, I never vomit just once. My body had to dry-heave five or six times to ensure my stomach had been turned inside out and thoroughly beaten like an old carpet.

Off to my left, the jeep's driver was talking to the woman standing in the middle of the road. Her dusty face had deep wrinkles in furrows across her forehead and bracketing her mouth like parentheses. Her lips caved in around her mouth, a sign she had no teeth. She was wearing layers of brown clothes, the outer layers looked like well-worn blankets turned into a poncho dress. She had to roasting in the jungle heat. She pointed back in the direction we'd just come from with a stubby finger and then adjusted her wide-brimmed hat.

Owen looked on from the back of the jeep. Ziggler, still seated in the front seat of the jeep, had seen me blowing chunks and held up a bottle of water.

I walked over and grabbed the bottle. "Thanks."

Ziggler held a hand up. "Don't bother giving it back."

I sipped and rinsed my mouth for few seconds before spitting the water back out. My stomach wasn't ready for anything, even a sip of water, but I had to clean the vomit taste out of my mouth.

Mila had climbed out of the truck while I was hiding my breakfast in the bushes and was now standing on the driver's side of the jeep near the woman.

"What's going on?" I asked no one in particular.

Owen leaned forward from the back seat of the jeep. "She's hard to understand. She might be Quechua, but she's not wearing the bright clothes of the women in Tarapoto," he said.

"She's confused," Mila said. "She says tourists take the other road at that last fork."

As Mila walked over to the jeep's driver, Owen waved to get her attention. "Tell her we aren't tourists. The people in Urycu are expecting us."

Not glancing back at Owen, Mila said something to the driver and then turned toward the old woman. She engaged her in conversation, but the woman just kept shaking her head. Eventually, she stepped aside while giving Mila and the rest of us a long, hard look.

Mila and I climbed back into the truck. I wanted to know what the two women had discussed, but Mila didn't offer any details as she told Shyla and Kat what had happened. At least she skipped the part about me launching my empanadas into the forest.

As the driver fired up the truck's engine, I peeked through the makeshift window to see the old woman looking up at me, her face a stone-faced stare. I gave her a little smile, but all she returned was a slow blink as she moved to the side of the road to let us pass.

Chapter 5

The town of Urycu was not much of a town, just a wide dirt road with a handful of side streets battling the encroaching jungle for space. Most of the buildings were made of concrete, but a few were wood. Rusty corrugated sheet metal poked out from under the edges of thatched roofs.

As we drove in, the locals halted their dance of life as if a needle had dragged across a record. People froze as they looked at us with curiosity and surprise. A weathered man leading a dilapidated burro pulling a ramshackle wood cart stood at the roadside, waiting for us to pass. A few old cars dotted the edge of the road, but for the most part, it looked like the people of Urycu walked everywhere.

It was as if we'd stumbled upon a lost city seemingly stuck in the 1950s—a place where time had little meaning. Life probably hadn't changed much during the past fifty years. I could dig it for a week.

We stopped in front of the local church. It appeared to be the nicest building in town, but by no means extravagant. Actually, I realized at second glance, it appeared nicer mostly because it wore the freshest coat of white paint and was one of the few buildings standing two stories tall. Like all the other buildings, though, little chunks of concrete had flaked off at the walls and corners. It was if the whole town had been through a war.

The church had two buildings attached to it. One was obviously a school, and the other was probably living quarters. It reminded me of the old church schoolhouses back in rural Wisconsin where I'd grown up.

Owen hopped out of the jeep and clapped his hands. "We're here!" he bellowed.

I hung back while Mila, Kat, and Shyla climbed out of the truck. I needed a few seconds to relish the stillness before hopping out. My residual nausea vanished the moment my feet hit solid ground.

A nun exited the school, smiling when she saw Owen. She moved as quickly and fluidly as a young person, but from the crow's feet at the corners of her eyes, I guessed she was in her late forties. She wasn't wearing a classic nun's habit, but instead an off-white tunic and matching cloth hat wrapped around her head. Her English sounded fluent, but she spoke so softly I could only make out snippets of what she was saying to Owen as I approached. She seemed grateful we'd made it, as if there was some doubt.

I did hear her say it had been ten years since medical help had been there, and something about the pathology being advanced. The way she spoke, it seemed clear she had nursing experience. No one outside the medical field would refer to townspeople with untreated diseases as advanced pathology.

Owen waved me over. "Rees Baker, this is Sister Torres. Rees is an ear, nose, and throat surgeon here on his first mission."

"Welcome, welcome, Doctor Baker," Sister Torres said.

"Just call me Rees," I said, offering my hand to Sister Torres. She gave it a good squeeze and then wrapped her other hand around mine, too, like she was giving me a sincere thank-you for work I hadn't done yet.

A giant raindrop splatted on my head as thick, heavy clouds had crowded out the blue sky overhead. Moments later, grape-sized raindrops began falling in earnest. They plopped to the ground and kicked up dust that quickly turned to mud. I seized the opportunity turn my face to the rain, closing my eyes as it washed the road dirt away.

Sister Torres called out orders in Spanish, and a second later, the two drivers began moving our bags from the truck to the school's entryway. We non–Spanish speakers took their cue and helped, while Sister Torres kept watch under the protection of the overhang by the front door. When the task was finished, the drivers climbed back into the vehicles and drove away.

As we all crowded under the overhang with Sister Torres to watch them go, Owen clapped his hands together and gave an evil laugh. "You're in my world now until they come back to get us next week."

I tried to wring out my shirt. "I wish your world was a little drier," I muttered.

Sister Torres smiled at me. "Welcome to the jungle, Dr. Rees. It rains almost every midday, but will finish as fast as it starts."

Next to me, Kat was rubbing her cell phone dry on her own shirt. "Do you have any signal?" she asked. "I can't tell if my phone's not working because it got wet or because we're out in the middle of nowhere."

I pulled out my own phone, which showed no service. "Nada," I told her.

Ooh, breaking out the Spanish. Muy bien, big boy.

Owen looked at us with no pity. "You two lost, wet kittens can survive a week without a phone."

Kat exaggerated a sigh and shoved the phone into her pocket. "I doubt it."

I powered mine down, too. No sense wasting the battery.

"C'mon, grab your bags," Owen said as Sister Torres waved us into the school.

Inside, the recently whitewashed concrete walls couldn't mask the wear and tear. Faded, chipped aquamarine tiles with a wavy pattern of lighter and darker blue covered the floor. Despite being well worn, every surface gleamed with cleanliness. Clearly, someone slaved to keep the otherwise dilapidated building so shiny.

Cleanliness is next to godliness, Lou reminded me.

"Do you remember the layout?" Sister Torres asked Owen.

He snapped his fingers and then tapped his temple. "These are the classrooms along this wall," he told us with a wave of his left hand. "And the hall on the right has three bedrooms in it. The last one is for the ladies . . . right?" Owen looked to Sister Torres, who nodded.

Owen turned to me. "You get a special room, Mr. Outdoors—all the way back, past the OR, and down a squiggly hallway.

Owen paused, looking around to make sure none of us had any questions. "Let's meet at the kitchen in ten. We've got to set up the OR and recovery room before we see some patients this afternoon. I want everything ready today so we can start doing cases first thing tomorrow morning," he said.

"Sir, yes sir," I said, snapping my heels to attention and saluting.

"One more word from you, Private, and you're going to be giving me twenty," Owen replied, spanking me as I separated from the rest of the group to find my room.

I stopped to peek into one of the classrooms. Mismatched child-sized chairs and desks had been pushed off to the side to make room for a couple of adult-sized benches. Our waiting room for the week, I assumed. I stepped inside for a closer look at the drawings of animals along one wall. As I skimmed them, I realized they were all of creatures American children could only hope to see in a zoo. Here in Peru, kids had a real chance of seeing macaws, sloths, alpacas, and even jaguars . . . all without bars around them. Despite the poor conditions of the town and the creepy-crawly things I knew were hiding out here, there was a certain allure to living in the jungle. The Amazon jungle, no less.

One of the drawings caught my eye. It was a black alligator walking upright, its open mouth showing off a rack of pointy teeth. Underneath was written the word "Nochedrilo." At first I thought this was the artist's name, but all the other drawings were labeled with the names of the animals depicted. I'd never heard of a nochedrilo.

Who cares about some bipedal crocodile? Let's go find a snack. I'm hungry.

"Cute pictures, huh?" Kat said from behind me.

"Yeah, except maybe this black alligator guy," I said.

Kat stepped next to me and shuddered. "I wouldn't want to bump into half the things on this wall."

I looked over at her. "What, don't you like nature?"

"I like nature as long as it stays in its place. You want to see an anaconda without a giant plate of glass holding it back?"

"I want to see everything," I replied. I pointed to a drawing of a poison dart frog. "See this little guy? He carries enough poison to kill ten humans."

Kat laughed. "Is he for hire?"

I like a girl who isn't afraid to have a frog do her dirty work.

Shyla poked her head in the door. "There you two are. Get a move on. Owen needs our help bringing the equipment to the OR."

As Kat followed Shyla back to their room, I made my way

through a dark, convoluted passageway to a storage area at the back of the school. Two doors were built into the back wall. Assuming the heavier-duty one led outside, I opened the other to find a modest room: my quarters for the week. This room seemed to be from a different era than the school and dining area and looked to be the church's original living quarters. Aged plaster, falling apart in places, covered the walls. The electrical wiring stapled to the wall was obviously a late addition.

I threw my bag onto the bed and then immediately headed back the way I came to find the others. The building was quite the compound.

I was the last one to get to the dining area, where Sister Torres had already put out drinks and snacks.

I joined the others already sitting at a table drinking sodas and eating fried plantain chips. "Is your room to your liking?" Sister Torres asked.

Owen tipped his soda in my direction. "Rees almost didn't come because he didn't want to have to sleep indoors. He'd be happy sleeping in a tree."

Sister Torres turned toward me, her face serious. "Please don't go into the jungle at night. It's dangerous. If you must go during the day, stay on the trails leading up the hill from town."

Her warning was stern enough to get everyone's attention. "Dangerous?" Ziggler asked.

Sister Torres picked up an empty glass from the table. "The jungle is full of hazards. During the day, you might spot a snake or wandering spider in time to avoid a poisonous encounter. At night, though, you'd never know what got you." This last part she said with the pleasantness of a third-grade teacher.

Kat shivered. "Wandering spiders?"

Sister Torres picked up a pitcher of water off the table with her other hand. "Oh yes, they can be deadly. They look similar to tarantulas. Don't touch any of the hairy spiders."

Kat shrunk back into her chair. "Don't worry, I won't touch *any* spiders."

"Clean-shaven or not," Owen muttered.

Sister Torres offered the glass and pitcher to me. "Iced tea?"

"Please," I said. "What's a nochedrilo?"

Sister Torres fumbled the glass in the air, only barely managing to save it before filling it with tea and handing it to me. "Ah, the Nochedrilo," she said, her smile plastic. "A child's tale. If you've been bad, the Night Crocodile will find you in the night and bite off a finger. The only way to escape is to fight, but if you lose, he eats you whole. When mothers catch their children in a lie, they warn, 'Better a finger than a head.' Better to admit it and give up something small before getting into bigger trouble."

These are some twisted people.

"I thought crocodiles were African," Shyla said.

Sister Torres smiled again, this time for real. "There are crocodiles in the Amazon, but we call them caiman. The Nochedrilo probably comes from the black caiman, which is the largest type and hunts at night."

Sister Torres left the room before any of us could ask another question. Kat raised an eyebrow at me, and I shrugged.

The good Sister Torres seemed pretty scared about a "child's tale."

Owen stood, drained the rest of his glass, and set it on the table. "Drink up, we've got a lot of work to do. Kat, you'll be helping Shyla in the recovery room, so the two of you can get started by setting that up." Kat looked like she was about to protest, but Owen shook his head. "You're welcome to come in the OR and see some cases after we get it rolling, but it's too technical for you to help set up."

Kat nodded in agreement that a deal had been made. She would go to the OR at some point. Ziggler and Shyla stood up and headed for the door with Kat just behind them. I needed just another minute's rest, no need to hurry. I finished my iced tea in a few long sips. I snatched a handful of salty fried corn kernels off the table. Those Peruvians like to snack like truck drivers. I liked it.

Together we carried the boxes of supplies we'd brought from the front door to the operating room in the back of the school. The OR was the last room before the narrow hallway that led back to my room. Inside, dust-covered tarps covered medical equipment and supplies that must have been left over from previous missions, maybe even from Owen's years before. The walls were painted concrete. One wall was filled with shelving covered by plastic sheets to prevent too much dust from getting onto whatever was being stored on them.

It wasn't an OR like back home. It was a storage room with an old ceiling-mounted surgical light. At the center of the room sat a sturdy metal relic of an OR table, with a series of large metal cranks on the side instead of the electric hand control of modern tables. Before the table showed up in this OR, it had probably been used to stretch poor souls to death in medieval times. Sister Torres could scare any naughty students straight with just a glimpse of this room.

Together, we all worked to get the room in shape, and a few hours later, we had the semblance of an OR. A medical mission OR is usually a far stretch from an American OR. Some missions are huge, allowing them to essentially rebuild their home OR abroad by transporting loads of supply and ample manpower. Our group was bare-bones. Ziggler had borrowed (without asking, I assumed) some surgical instruments from our hospital, condensing them into small but complete sets: hernia, appendectomy, soft-tissue excision, abdominal. By timing things right, we could perform an operation on one patient while the instruments we'd need for the next were being sterilized.

We lacked a real ventilator, but Owen could manually "bag" patients. This meant hand-squeezing a rubber bag to force oxygen through the endotracheal tube and into patients' lungs while they were under anesthesia. "It's good exercise," he claimed, pumping his fist a few times as proof. "Hand-bagging in a place like this is better than a real ventilator, anyway, since the electricity isn't always reliable."

I looked up from the supplies I was organizing. "Surgery without electricity?"

Owen read the look on my face. "Don't worry, the OR light has a battery backup."

"Real surgeons don't need light," I said.

Owen smiled. "Yeah, just like the old days. Surgery by candlelight."

Candlelight? By feel.

Owen popped up from the chair he'd been resting in and headed to the door. "C'mon, let's go find some disease to stamp out."

***

Owen and I joined Shyla at the front of the school, where she was already seeing patients. The school's classrooms were serving as our waiting, exam, and recovery rooms, and the waiting room was already packed. Sister Torres had apparently been busy rounding up our patients in town while we'd been setting up the OR.

Shyla met me at the door. "I saw a guy with huge nasal polyps. He'll come back tomorrow to see you. I already have a couple surgical candidates for you for tomorrow morning." She gestured at the fifteen or so people waiting on benches along the wall. Most of them looked like small families. Almost everyone wore short-sleeved cotton shirts—some T-shirts, some blouses. Nothing particularly ethnic. And nothing as layered or gloomy as the spooky old woman we passed on the way here.

A scrawny boy, three or four years old and wearing a faded red T-shirt, sat on the floor playing with a handmade cloth doll. When he looked up at me with wide brown eyes, he let the doll fall limp.

Not too often he sees a tall, ugly, bald dude. Stick your tongue out at him.

I winked instead. The boy smiled and went back to his toy.

"This is just a couple patients?" I asked.

Shyla patted me on the shoulder as if to reassure me and then waved at the boy. "Luis?"

The skinny boy with the doll looked up. I expected him to run or cry or at least hide behind his mom like so many kids do back home, but instead he smiled proudly. He probably never got to see doctors...and their needles.

Two women sitting on the bench near Luis stood up. One was clearly Mom, and the other maybe an aunt. They all followed us into the next room, where we sat on benches. There was a small bed waiting to be used as an examining table, but I let Luis sit on the bench next to his mom.

Right away I noticed he never closed his mouth. Most people breathe through their nose at rest, especially when seated, so this gave me a clue about why he was there. His bony shoulders made corners in his T-shirt, not because the shirt was too big but because his arms were too small. "Failure to thrive" is what we call it when kids aren't the size expected for their age, suggesting some form of malnutrition. That was the phrase I thought of looking at Luis. I could probably wrap my finger and thumb clear around his bicep.

"How old is he?" I asked Shyla so she could translate.

Shyla bent toward Luis. "Cuántos años?"

Luis smiled and looked down shyly. He held out his hand with all five fingers showing.

"Cinco?" Shyla asked. Luis looked younger, but Mom smiled and nodded.

Although Shyla could speak Spanish well, she barely introduced me. Normally a patient interaction starts with introductions, a discussion of the problem, and moves on to an exam. But in old-school medicine, the doctor merely walks into the room, looks at what's wrong, and states the treatment. Shyla converted to paternalistic mission mode before I even knew what was happening, asking Luis to sit on his mom's lap and open his mouth, and then pushing a flashlight into my hand.

When Mom patted her lap for Luis to sit, I noticed that half of her left middle finger was missing. Forget about the romance of living as one with the animals; life in the jungle was apparently rough.

Yeah, she probably lost that finger to a piranha for lunch.

Luis hopped onto his mom's lap and proudly opened his mouth. My flashlight immediately illuminated kissing tonsils, the nickname for tonsils so large they touch, blocking both airway and esophagus. That explained Luis's constant struggle to breathe. It's not common for giant tonsils to be the sole cause of failure to thrive, but it can happen. Luis probably burned half his calories just grinding his food into liquid to slip it past the blockade.

I excused myself to go find Owen, who was in the operating room tinkering with the oxygen tank for his hand-powered ventilator. "Can we do a tonsil on a tiny five-year-old?"

Owen didn't even bother looking up. "Of course. I could intubate a baby. You have what you need?"

"I think so. I mean I don't have the ideal stuff, but I can make do."

Owen chuckled. "That's the attitude. But check that box over there." He jerked his thumb at a cardboard box along the wall.

I opened it to find a few tonsillectomy tools, including the most important, an apparatus that holds the patient's mouth open, tongue down, and endotracheal tube out of the way.

"This isn't my first rodeo, you know," Owen said.

"Well, it's mine. I owe you one," I replied.

Now Owen looked up. "You're here. That means I owe you more than one."

On my way back to Luis, I spotted Kat in another classroom, handing out little boxes of crayons to some kids. They were ecstatic, and Kat's face reflected their excitement. She didn't look anything like the woman I'd seen onstage in YouTube videos. This Kat had the same nurturing look I often saw on Shyla as we worked. More than that, this Kat looked happy.

As I walked away, I realized I probably looked happy, too.

***

After seeing more patients, we closed the clinic for the evening and met in the dining area attached to the kitchen and living quarters near the front of the church. Open windows covered with mosquito netting comprised most of the front wall. Religious pictures adorned the other walls. A suffering Jesus sculpture hanging on the back wall slightly disturbed me. The bloody man on the cross sucked the festivity out of the room.

This guy fed himself to the sharks for your sins. The least you can do is tip your hat to his bloody, tortured carcass on the wall.

As night fell, Sister Torres lit candles even though the electricity worked. A breeze worked its way through the netting and cooled our weary crew.

43

Shyla and Kat entered last, and the reason was immediately obvious. Both of them sparkled, whereas Owen, Ziggler and I were still roughed up from the truck ride. Shyla's hair glistened with water. She and Kat wore fresh short-sleeved shirts with floral designs, not identical but close enough to make me wonder if they'd coordinated their packing.

Owen fanned his face. "You two look like you just finished a revitalizing spa afternoon."

Kat smiled, crossed her arms, and rubbed her biceps with her hands in an exaggerated shiver. "Oh, yes. We've started our eight-day cold-water cleanse."

"*Eight whole days,*" Ziggler whined as if mocking her, before continuing in a normal voice. "The locals get to look forward to an entire life of cold showers."

Kat flashed Ziggler a snarl and slid into the chair farthest from him. Shyla took the one next to her.

Owen cleared his throat and rapped his cup on the table twice. "No bickering in Peru. Let's talk business." His stern tone matched his words. "The first thing we'll do each night at dinner is talk about the next day's cases and anything else we need to be prepared for. After that, we'll drink beer and eat and relax." He pointed to two boxes in the corner bearing the label *Cusqueña*, a Peruvian beer. "Did I mention we'll drink beer?"

He gave us a chance to cheer before continuing. "Tomorrow we start with the tonsillectomy. Just like home, the youngest patient goes first unless there's a more compelling case. Any concerns, Rees?"

I shook my head.

As Owen spoke, Sister Torres made three trips into the dining room to bring in large pots of beans and rice and chicken. Owen paused as she put down the last one, and she pointed at our meal. "The food is simple, but on the last night we'll have a party and serve guinea pig. It's a delicacy here in Peru."

As Kat and Shyla widened their eyes in unison, I realized Owen's earlier comment about not having a choice of what to eat wasn't a joke. This was going to be both a geographical and gastronomical adventure.

Is a guinea pig a gopher? Well, I can't gopher that . . . no can do.

Put a cork in it, Hall and Oates.

While we ate, Sister Torres explained a bit of her history with the church and the school. She'd been born in France, moved to the United States, and later settled in Peru. Her mission in life was to bring God and education to this remote town.

I don't think I could give up fresh-baked croissants for the jungle life.

I watched Sister Torres closely as I ate. She'd sacrificed her whole life for this entirely different one in Urycu. If she could do it for decades, I could do it for a week. Maybe I didn't need backpacking in the Sierras at all. I could hardly wait to get started in the OR the next morning.

When Sister Torres finished, Owen raised his glass. "Cheers, everyone. Thanks for donating your time and effort to make this a successful mission. And as Sister Torres said and Axl Rose sang, welcome to the jungle."

Toward the end of the meal, an older man wearing a black button-up shirt and black jeans stepped into the room, and Sister Torres rose to introduce him. "This is Dr. Yanpa, a doctor down in the valley."

While Sister Torres pulled out a chair at the end of our table for him, I took a closer look at our local colleague. He was probably in his fifties, with streaks of silver in his hair like strands of tinsel and deep-set eyes hidden under a large brow. Pockmarks covered his face. Vertical wrinkles interrupted his brow as if he spent his life glowering. His tight lips looked like he was holding back a scowl at the very moment.

He looks like the type of guy who'd stab his mother in the back.

Sister Torres pointed to us in order. "This is Dr. Jacobsen, Dr. Ziggler, and Dr. Rees."

I smiled. Sister Torres still didn't realize Rees was my first name, not my last.

Dr. Yanpa took his seat. He exchanged a few quick words in

Spanish with Sister Torres. She glanced at us and left the room without a word.

Dr. Yanpa looked at Owen. "Sister Torres tells me you are the leader of the group, Dr. Jacobsen," he said in English.

"I am," Owen answered. "These are the other two members of our team, Shyla and Kat."

Dr. Yanpa gave them a brief nod. He slowly folded his hands together as if they were delicate and he wasn't sure they would fit. The last two joints of the last two fingers on his left hand were missing. Apparently, Luis's mom wasn't the only person who'd lost parts of fingers to life in the jungle.

Dr. Yanpa turned from Shyla and Kat back to Owen. "Where are you from?"

"California," Owen answered in an uncharacteristically flat voice. His face seemed tense, but I wasn't sure why.

Sister Torres brought out a glass of water for Dr. Yanpa, set it down, and immediately disappeared again.

Dr. Yanpa gave us all a slow look. "The food here is good?"

We nodded, waiting for him to get to the point. He wasn't joining us just to shoot the breeze.

"Very good. Very good," Dr. Yanpa said. "But you must be careful how you treat people here."

"Of course. We'll do the best we can," Owen said.

Dr. Yanpa frowned. "Maybe you shouldn't."

We all exchanged looks. What was going on?

Dr. Yanpa continued. "People here are used to a certain way of life. I am their doctor. As you have your routines with your patients in California, I have my routines here. These are people with limited resources. What do you think happens when you come here and work miracles for free?"

The way the words came out of Dr. Yanpa's mouth, it sounded like our group was stealing rather than giving. Owen laughed. "People get better."

Dr. Yanpa didn't look amused. "They do, but when you fix what usually can't be fixed, you hurt the rest of them. You hurt me. In a few weeks when you are back in California, someone here will need an operation. When I can't help them and they don't have the money to go to Tarapoto, I will be the man who can't do anything, while the Americans, they could do everything and charge nothing. What do you think that will that do to my practice?"

Ziggler leaned toward him. "What exactly are you trying to say?"

Dr. Yanpa's knuckles turned white as he squeezed his glass. "I have been here for decades. I will be here after you leave. Let our routine be your routine."

I never would have imagined a local doctor being unhappy about surgeons coming to help his town. Dr. Yanpa wanted us to do less than our best, just to make himself look good.

Owen shook his head. "No can do, Doc. We're here to help people. You took the same oath. Maybe you should stick around and work with us. We might even be able to teach you a few things you can use after we leave."

Shyla gave Owen a slight smile of approval.

Dr. Yanpa's dark eyes narrowed to slits. "I am not going to work for you. These are *my* people. You should work for *me*. You should pay *me* for the privilege of operating on my patients."

Owen's mouth dropped open. "Huh?"

Dr. Yanpa nodded. "I think two thousand dollars is a fair price."

Kat jerked upright in her chair. "We're not paying you to take care of people!"

Dr. Yanpa stood up abruptly, setting his water glass down with a thud. "You *will* pay me." He huffed a few deep breaths and clenched his jaw. "I will return in three days to collect. You should either have the money or be gone."

He stormed out the door and we all turned to Owen, who wasn't even trying to mask his disappointment. "This shit happens on medical missions," he reassured us. "It's not the first time someone's asked me for a payoff. But don't worry, that chump's not getting a dime."

Shyla shuddered. "But that sounded like a threat."

"He's all talk," Ziggler said. "What's he going to do, send the

47

Nochedrilo after us?"

Sister Torres appeared in the doorway. "Careful what you say. Dr. Yanpa is not a good man."

Her comment silenced the room. So much for the relaxing, chatting, and beer drinking Owen had promised.

"Can't you do anything?" Shyla asked Sister Torres.

Before Sister Torres could respond, Owen stood and put a hand on her shoulder. "Sister Torres has to live here after we're gone. We need to settle this so she doesn't have to worry about retribution."

Sister Torres put her hand on top of his, obviously relieved. Owen gave her a smile and then looked at the rest of us. "We'll figure it out tomorrow. Right now, we need sleep."

While everyone else retired to their rooms inside the building, I dragged my carcass outside to get to mine. The sky was still pink with the setting sun and I tried to perk up for the short walk so I didn't look weak or drunk in front of any locals who might be watching.

My batteries were dead, though, and that exhaustion fueled my irritation. I couldn't fathom the gall it had taken Dr. Yanpa to ask us—*threaten us*—for money. But Owen was right. Sleep first.

The walk to my room confirmed my earlier suspicion. The church had likely been built first, with my room as the original living quarters behind it. As the years passed, the school had been built next to the church, and the space between the two buildings was filled with additional living quarters, storage, and the dining area.

Owen had also been right about going outside to get to my room instead of through the winding corridor inside.

Admit it, the storage area gave you the creeps.

Sure did.

The part of the building housing my room sat at the dead end of a narrow dirt street, behind the church and right next to the jungle. A thin path cutting through the jungle vegetation invited me in. I couldn't wait to explore after a good night's sleep and a hefty coating of bug repellent.

I entered my room from the street and flicked the light switch. A dull yellow 40-watt bulb illuminated two cots and a table with a chair, the room's only furniture. At least it had its own bathroom. When I turned on the bathroom light, a large beetle ran across the shower floor and down the drain hole, which lacked a drain basket to catch hair or block beetles. I ran the water for a minute to wash away my roommate, but skipped a shower for myself out of fear the cold water would wake me.

After washing the last remnants of the drive's dirt from my face and brushing my teeth, I arranged a rolled-up T-shirt, a pair of shorts, flip-flops, and a flashlight on the floor next to the head of the bed, my habit when sleeping while on call. Be prepared to go at any time. An ex-girlfriend used to tease me about it, saying it looked less like danger-preparedness and more like I was getting ready for an impromptu midnight pool party. Her jokes stopped after a three a.m. fire alarm sent us running out of our hotel room one night.

I flopped onto the bed. Seconds before I fell asleep, there was a gentle rap on the door.

"One sec," I called as I threw on the T-shirt and pair of shorts while mentally patting myself on the back for taking the time to set them out. I opened the door a crack to find Owen peeking back at me.

"You naked?" Owen asked.

I opened the door for him. "Nope."

Owen pushed his way into the room. "Too bad. I promised the crew back home I'd post nudie shots of you on Facebook."

I yawned. "How about some of me sound asleep?"

"Yeah, yeah, this will only take a sec." He held out a small bag. "Take this. It's the extra morphine and some other supplies."

I took the bag, but frowned. "You don't really think Kat's got a problem, do you?"

Owen shook his head. "She might be a handful, but she's no junkie. Ziggler's overreacting."

I pushed the bag back to him. "So, you keep it."

He pushed back. "I told you, this isn't my first rodeo. The whole town knows we have drugs. The anesthesiologist's bag is the first place any thieves would look."

I wiggled the bag in his face. "How do you know I'm not a junkie?"

"Oh, please. The guy who won't drink caffeine because it makes him jittery?" Owen made his hands quiver to mock me as he walked back out the door. *"I'm a delicate surgeon. Don't give me a piece of chocolate before I operate, or the theophylline might make me twitchy."*

I slammed the door behind him, hearing him laugh as he walked away.

Hey, numbnuts, maybe you should try some of that morphine right now just to prove him wrong.

Yeah, right.

Just kidding. Take a chill pill. You need some sleep, Grumpy.

I stashed the bag of morphine in the mini medical kit I always take with me on vacation, jammed full of the basics for wound care and other minor surgical emergencies. One of my many security blankets.

Then I leapt into bed, not even bothering to remove my T-shirt and shorts before falling into a solid sleep.

Chapter 6

What are you doing?

Sleeping...

It doesn't seem like it. It seems like you're lying awake.

No. I'm exhausted. Let me sleep.

You fell asleep hours ago.

It's still dark out. It's not time to wake up yet.

But there's something scratching. It's creepy. Listen.

I sat perfectly still with my eyes closed. Sure enough, a faint *scratch, scratch, scratch*, like fingernails on a stone wall emanated from the front corner of the room. It stopped for a few beats and started again. What sort of weird creatures snoop around at night in Peru?

The Nochedrilo.

If that was the Nochedrilo, it sounded like it was ten inches tall. Not that a little black crocodile wouldn't be scary in itself. Just not as scary as a *big* black crocodile. But if it wasn't a little crocodile, what was it? More importantly, what alternative would I find tolerable? Would it be okay if whatever was in my room had claws, just as long as it couldn't move very fast? Or okay if it moved fast, just as long as it moved fast right out the door?

I reached down and grabbed the flashlight. As soon as my fingers felt the cold steel, I pulled my arm back into the bed, just in case there were other things in the room, too. Monsters under the bed.

I snapped the light on. It lit up the yellow walls and tile floor, but no Nochedrilo, or anything else. I scanned the light across the room. Still nothing.

Scratch, scratch, scratch.

I swung the light back to the front corner of the room.

Scratch, scratch.

Whatever was scratching was outside.

Go see what it is.

No way. It's out there. We're in here. The world is in harmony.

You'll never fall asleep unless you know what it is.

You suck.

I got out of bed and crept to the front door. I yanked it open and aimed my flashlight in the direction of the noise. A skinny gray cat looked up at me with disdain. When it realized I wasn't danger, it looked back at the wall and resumed scratching. After a couple unrewarding swipes, it turned and ran away.

I forced a weak smile as if I'd known all along it was just a cat. Getting all worked up over pint-sized crocodiles. Sissy.

I walked to where the cat had been scratching and pointed the flashlight on an inch-wide crack in the building's foundation. Something the cat wanted for dinner was undoubtedly hiding in that crack. A mouse, maybe, but I wasn't going to bend down and shine the light in there to find out. What if it was a tiny crocodile after all?

The low growling of a truck engine caught my ear. The idling engine seemed out of place in a town with so few cars, especially at this time of night. I covered the flashlight with my hand to dim it and then walked to the edge of the building to peek. Men were shuffling, half asleep, into the back of an old truck parked at the front corner of the school. Maybe they worked in Tarapoto and made the long trip every morning?

A short man in a black jacket and pants stood near the back of the truck. He grabbed one of the last guys in line and gave him a sharp slap across the face, hard enough that I heard it echo. The slapped guy didn't flinch, but he stood tall to hold his ground.

Another man stepped up next to the short man in black, something shiny in his hand. Was it a gun?

The taller man who had just been slapped took a step backward. There was some sort of harsh conversation I could barely hear. The man with the shiny object moved forward.

The three of them stood still for a moment as I watched in morbid awe to see what would happen next.

The tall man lowered into a fighting stance, as did the short man who had slapped him. The man with the shiny thing moved back.

The taller one rushed the shorter one, and I heard a series of thumps and grunts. When the tall man fell to the ground, the shorter one started kicking him. Hard. Repeatedly.

I'm all for helping a fellow man, but stay away from this one.

When the man on the ground stopped moving, the short man walked to the front of the truck. Three men hopped out of the back of the truck, scooped up the tall man, and pulled him into the truck with them.

Something is not right here, I almost said out loud as the truck pulled away.

No shit, Sherlock.

If I'd been at home in California, I would've called the police. But whom could I call out here in the jungle? Even if I knew, I didn't have cell service.

This tiny town was floating in the middle of an ocean of greenery. What could the townspeople do about a shark-like bully apparently picking them off one at a time?

Back in my room, I tried to sleep at least another hour, but there was no rest to be found after what I'd just seen.

***

When little Luis arrived a few hours later for his surgery, his mom was clearly trying to hold her worry behind a nervous smile and taut face. Luis beamed like he'd won a prize.

"The operating room is ready, Dr. Rees," Sister Torres said.

I nodded my head toward Luis. "Why is he smiling so much? My young patients in America are usually scared to have surgery."

Sister Torres smiled. "I told him he was very lucky. He gets to be the first patient the American doctors help."

I looked at Luis and gave him a wink. "I'll have to start telling my patients back home how lucky they are. Is Owen ready?"

"Yes, Doctor," Sister Torres answered.

I gave Luis and his mother a thumbs up. "All right, let's go."

Sister Torres immediately turned and spouted something in Spanish so fast I couldn't pick up a single word. Luis hopped off his bed and took her hand, and his mother followed them down the hallway.

Taking out tonsils is like peeling masking tape off cardboard. With just the right tension, the strip comes off whole. Pull too hard, and it tears.

Once Owen out Luis to sleep, I injected the palate and arches just lateral to the tonsils with a lidocaine and epinephrine mixture. Lidocaine to numb Luis's nerves, and epinephrine to constrict the blood vessels around his tonsils.

Starting a case is very much a tortoise-and-hare sort of race. It's in a surgeon's nature to get things going. I've never licked my way to the center of a Tootsie Pop, like that old commercial goes.

Darn tootin'. Quit your blabbing and let's unzip those tonsils so we can get on with the next case.

It takes four minutes for epinephrine to have maximum effect, so I injected the anesthetic mix into Luis before Sister Torres had finished getting the rest of the surgical tools ready for the case. "Do we have any catheters?" I asked Owen as I waited. When I do tonsillectomies on kids back home, I normally pass a urinary catheter into my patient's right nostril and pull the other end out their mouth. Then I loosely tie it so it holds the palate tight. This provides both a better view of the top part of the tonsil and a little counter-traction.

Owen squeezed the bag he was using to manually breathe for Luis, forcing air into the boy's lungs through the endotracheal tube. "Catheters are in short supply," he said. "We need to save them for any patients with urinary retention."

I looked around the room for any alternative that might work. "What about the second limb of his IV tubing?"

IV tubing has three ends, one that goes into the patient's bloodstream from the main bag, plus two that allow "piggyback" IV bags of antibiotics or other medications to flow in simultaneously. But Luis didn't need IV antibiotics, so he didn't need the second limb of his IV tube, either.

Owen looked over at Sister Torres. "You have a spare scissors and clamp?" She handed him scissors. Owen tied off and then cut the second limb of IV tubing closest to its division. Just to be safe, he clamped the tied end to prevent air from getting sucked into the line and Luis's veins.

After Owen wiped the loose tube with an alcohol wipe and handed it to me, I cut the hub off the other end to create a perfect, flexible tube. This passed easily into Luis's nose, and, with a few pushes, the tube turned the corner and popped into view in the back of his throat. I retrieved it with a long forceps and tied it into place.

"Nice improvisation," Owen said. He turned to Sister Torres. "See, I told you he'd be great."

"I haven't done anything yet," I said.

"It's called getting shit done," Owen replied and then smiled sheepishly. "Um, sorry Sister."

Sister Torres's eyes squinted with a smile that was otherwise hidden by her surgical mask.

Owen looked over at me. "You have no idea how much some of your colleagues back home whine and complain if everything isn't exactly how they want it. The staff runs in circles trying to find a left-handed thing-a-ma-bob, and by the time they find one half an hour later, the case could have been finished."

I adjusted my improvised fix. "So why bring Ziggler? He seems like the curmudgeonly kind who'd complain for half an hour."

Owen laughed. "He's a total curmudgeon, but he's my favorite curmudgeon. He likes to grouse, but just watch, he takes great care of people. Under that gruff exterior is a solid man."

"Solid?" I asked.

"Yes."

"Technically, he's mostly liquid." I watched Owen for a reaction.

Owen sighed. "You make a better surgeon than comedian. Now get operating."

I always operate wearing surgical loupes, which magnify my vision two-and-a-half times. Tonsils are easy enough to see without them, but I like a closer view of every little blood vessel. I grabbed Luis's right tonsil with a clamp and pulled it toward the left side. Then, with a light buzz of the electrocautery, I zapped the lining just lateral to his tonsil and cut down to the tonsil tissue that normally hides out of sight when you open your mouth wide.

Tonsils are attached directly to muscles used with every swallow.

Inflamed muscles don't like flexing, hence the painful post-operative recovery after a tonsillectomy. But there's a tissue-paper-thin white layer separating the tonsil from the muscle. If the surgeon's dissection stays on the surface of the tonsil, that's where the unzipping happens, allowing the tonsil to be peeled free from the muscle with just a push. With the tip of my electrocautery doing the pushing, I cauterized every tiny blood vessel I came across as I operated on Luis, and in about a minute, his right tonsil was out.

Most people don't know this, but a removed tonsil is exactly the size of a piece of sushi.

You could put it on a patty of rice, wrap a strip of seaweed around it, and serve it as nigiri. Of course, you'd have to be some sort of sick-ass cannibal to do that, but you could.

I removed Luis's second tonsil and Owen woke him up without a problem. Luis was peaceful and sleepy, no pain yet because the local anesthetic was keeping him numb. We moved him to a cot in the recovery room, which was just the classroom closest to the operating room. Ziggler had a hernia case following the tonsillectomy, and while he performed his surgery, I watched Shyla teach Kat how to take care of post-operative patients, in this case Luis.

Luis was still numb from the local anesthetic and groggy from whatever concoction Owen had given him, so post-operative care was more about watching him sleep. Shyla and Kat stood at the foot of his bed while his mom sat in a chair next to it, shifting as if a bit unnerved. She was used to the sounds of Luis's rough breathing. Without his tonsils blocking his airway, this was probably the first time he'd slept without snoring or gasping. Based on how carefully she watched his chest movements, the quiet probably made her worry Luis wasn't breathing at all. Our monitors did the watching for us and his oxygen level was just fine.

I left to grab a bottle of water, and when I returned, Shyla handed me a small flashlight. "I have the guy with the giant nasal polyp in the clinic."

I slipped the light into my chest pocket. "All right, let's take a look."

Kat stepped up with an eagerness usually reserved for children at the entrance of an amusement park. "Can I come see it?"

"Of course," I said, glancing at Shyla.

She waved us away. "Go on. I'll stay here and watch Luis."

When I Kat and I entered our makeshift waiting room, a handful of patients sitting on the benches looked at us. Waiting by the door was a stocky young man with thick, matted black hair.

"Hello, Doctor," he squeaked in a characteristic hyponasal voice. Not much air moving through those nostrils.

"Hola," I replied.

"Cómo te llamas?" Kat asked.

I gave her a glance. If she could help translate, she was already worth having around.

"Pedro," the man answered.

"Soy Kat y es Doctor Rees," Kat said. She turned to me and whispered, "Sorry, I only know textbook Spanish."

"Then forget about translating," I told her. "I'll go back to hand gestures and repeating things extra loud and super slow in English."

She smiled.

"Ree-es," Pedro repeated.

"Yo escucho que su nariz está bloqueada," Kat said.

Textbook Spanish? Muthaflippin' dictionary.

Pedro tilted his nose toward me and tried to breathe in. A tiny whistle of air wiggled the whitish, translucent polyp nearly protruding from his right nostril.

I pulled the flashlight from my pocket and clicked it on. The light illuminated a semitransparent yellow polyp in his left nostril, too, further back than on the right and totally obstructing the passage.

"Abre la boca," I said, without the accent Kat or the Peruvians used. That one little sentence exhausted all the medical Spanish I was comfortable using in this conversation.

When Pedro opened his mouth, I could see the bottom of the glistening polyp obstructing his nasal passage.

"See that?" I asked Kat, pointing the light so she could see the polyp in the back of his mouth just behind his uvula, that little thing that hangs down like a punching bag.

She peeked past my shoulder. "What?"

"See how the polyp is filling his nose and hanging down in the back of his throat?" I looked at Pedro. "Say 'Aaahhhh,' por favor."

When Pedro followed the command, the polyp came into better view. Kat's chin touched my shoulder as she tried to get a better look. She smelled like cherry blossoms.

"Cool," she said, in an enthusiastic way that made me miss working with medical residents. I enjoyed the company of people eager to learn. Maybe that was something to look into once I was back home. There were a couple residency programs and medical schools in the area. Something to think about, at least.

Pedro didn't need the OR for treatment, just a place out of sight of the other people in the waiting area so what I was about to do wouldn't shock them. Kat brought him to the recovery room while I put on my mask and stopped in the operating room for supplies.

Ziggler was throwing the final stitches into the surgical wound from his hernia case. Sister Torres stood across the bed from him holding scissors, waiting to cut the suture.

Owen looked up from the head of the bed. "What's up?"

"I could use some local," I said. "I'm about to pluck out a giant nasal polyp."

Owen nodded. "What do you need?"

"Cocaine would be ideal," I replied. "Too bad we aren't in Colombia."

Owen looked up at Sister Torres. "There's plenty of cocaine here in Peru, right, Sister?"

Sister Torres's wide eyes fixed on him. "We don't talk about that, Dr. Owen."

Sister Torres turned to me. "Is cocaine a drug doctors use?" Her question bore the same skeptical curiosity of a little kid asking if Santa were real. She wanted to believe, but in her heart, she knew the truth.

"I'm sure a bunch of doctors use it," Ziggler chuckled under his mask.

"I wasn't joking. It has its place," I assured her. "It's the only local anesthetic that also constricts blood vessels, so I use it to numb noses."

"You shouldn't mention it to the patients," Sister Torres said. "It won't be understood."

I turned back to Owen. "How about some lido with epi instead?"

Owen plucked a bottle out of his bag and tossed it to me. "Be sure to save the leftovers."

Back in the recovery room, I sat in a little chair facing Pedro, who was sitting on the edge of the cot with a blue surgical towel draped around his chest like a bib at a crab feast. Shyla set up a small instrument tray on my right side to hold a few of my "toys."

With Kat looking over my shoulder, I injected the polyp with anesthetic. I squirted what was left in the syringe onto some strips of pulled-apart cotton balls.

"What causes nasal polyps?" Kat asked.

I stuck the cotton inside Pedro's nose. "It's a mystery. Some are a certain type of tumor, but most are just bad luck, an exuberant inflammatory reaction."

Kat leaned in closer, and I smelled cherry blossoms again. "I suppose that's what surgery's about. Just cut out things you don't know how to fix with medicine."

I arranged my instruments while we waited for the anesthetic to work. "In this case, you're right. Cutting out polyps is like cutting weeds in a garden. The roots stay behind, so it's wait-and-see as to how fast they grow back."

Kat's "mmm-hmm" reply left me with the impression she was tucking the idea of finding a better cure for nasal polyps into her to-do list somewhere between doing her laundry and recording a new album. Her curiosity about all things medical surprised me, although it made sense considering her sister being a nurse.

Five minutes later, Pedro's nose was as numb as it was going to get. I put the headlight on, grabbed a nasal speculum, and spread his left nostril open as far as it would go. Polyp filled his nose. With my other hand, I used an instrument with a small grasper at the end to push around the polyp.

Kat leaned in even closer and I nodded with my chin. "The polyp's root is either on the sidewall of his nasal passage, underneath a cleft, or coming from up high," I explained.

Pulling the polyp forward didn't do anything but obstruct my view, so I went to plan B and started pushing it backward. Pedro's whole body leaned backward with the pressure. Since we didn't have an exam chair with a rigid headrest to prevent his reflex to back away, Shyla put her hand on his upper back as a reminder to hold still.

Kat whispered into my ear, "Why aren't you pulling it out?"

"I'm trying to find its stalk," I whispered back, spying a narrowing of the polyp at the top edge as I pushed. "Look, it's coming from a shelf of tissue on the sidewall of the nose." I moved my head aside but kept the light in Pedro's nose so Kat could look.

I grabbed the stalk as high up as I could with my grasper and gently pulled down. If I could pull off the lining the stalk was growing from, it might not grow back. The stalk came loose, so I grabbed the polyp and pulled. When it didn't budge, I pulled harder until it started to tear where the grasper was holding.

One of the lessons subtly taught in medical school is how to keep a straight face when things aren't going exactly as planned. Part two of that lesson is to continue moving forward while silently hemming and hawing about the real next step so the patient doesn't get suspicious. As I struggled to remove the polyp, Kat and Shyla watched eagerly. Luis was awake now, too, and he sat tall on his knees on his cot, like a prairie dog getting a look over the tall grasses, as he and his family also watched to see what would come out of Pedro's nose.

As long as I kept the speculum in Pedro's nose and wiggled the polyp a little, it looked like I was doing something productive. The last thing I wanted to do was pull the polyp out piecemeal. Where's the thrill in that? But clearly this baby was too big for a standard delivery, and a C-section wasn't an option. I needed to stall while I figured out a better solution.

You can always try the back door, numbnuts.

Not exactly how I'd phrase it, but yes.

I gently pushed the polyp backward with the grasper, and it didn't resist. With a few gentle pushes, I moved it to the back half of the nasal passage. I stopped before going too far, I didn't want choke Pedro.

I removed the nasal speculum and instructed Pedro to open his mouth. Kat gasped when she saw the polyp hanging prominently in his throat. As Pedro said, "ahhhh," I reached in and got a good hold of the polyp. Then, with one solid pull, I delivered the polyp from the back of Pedro's nose and out of his mouth.

I slapped the polyp, about half the size of a deck of cards, onto the instrument tray. It looked like a giant glob of chicken fat, shiny and yellow, with a few streaks of blood on it. It looked like an alien larva.

"Holy shit!" Kat said under her breath.

"Wow," Shyla said.

Pedro wobbled like he was going to pass out. He straightened up and closed his mouth and took a deep sniff, his first sniff in years. His smile lit up his face, and Luis clapped in approval as he and his family stared incredulously at the monstrous polyp.

"Ta-da," I said, not knowing if magician's words cross cultures. Nothing made medicine more rewarding than a quick, life-changing fix.

Kat smiled in approval.

Never thought such an ugly thing could make a pretty girl smile so widely.

Yeah, it is ugly. And yeah, she is pretty.

Kat and I walked Pedro back to the waiting area, where I asked her to tell him to stay for half an hour in case his nose bled after the anesthetic wore off. He probably wouldn't have any pain from the procedure since polyps just aren't nervy, but I also asked Kat to tell him to come back for Tylenol if he needed anything.

Pleased with the outcome of my second successful case, I took a quick breather in the classroom-turned-waiting area before going to see my next patient. I scanned the animal pictures on the wall again, wondering if Luis had drawn one of them, maybe even the one of the fearsome Nochedrilo.

But as I looked for that curious drawing again, my happiness turned to confusion. Where was the picture of the Nochedrilo? I was certain it had been in the center of the wall, but a picture of a snake was hanging in its place. I looked at every single picture on the wall again, with no luck. The Nochedrilo was definitely gone. But why?

As I left the waiting area to start my next case, I couldn't stop thinking about the drawing. Sister Torres had seemed worried when I'd asked about it the night before. Was she the one who'd taken the picture down? That seemed an overreaction to my innocent question.

My thoughts went back to the street fight I'd witnessed early that morning. There was an undercurrent here in Urycu. Something was happening, something we visitors knew nothing about. And as much as I didn't understand how or why, my instincts were telling me that the picture of the Nochedrilo was somehow connected.

Chapter 7

I thought it was generous enough just coming to Peru to operate on people in need, but no, there was more. We'd also apparently brought along a box loaded with deflated soccer balls, a few deflated volleyballs, and a hand pump.

We spent some time after lunch gift-giving. As the "young man" of the group, I was assigned to pump up the balls while the rest of the group handed them out to the kids. Ziggler mostly sat, paced, watched, sat, and paced some more. He finally gave in when a little boy kicked a ball to him. He smiled and kicked it back. The boy interpreted this as an invitation to continue.

Shyla had me pump up a volleyball about three-fourths of the way to keep it soft for the littlest kids.

I watched the kids playing while I pumped. "Owen's impressive. Were you part of his plan to bring the balls? And can I donate to the cause?"

Shyla picked up the volleyball. "Actually, Kat did it all. She organized the donation long before she ever decided to come along."

Of all the news Kat had generated over the years, I didn't remember any about her being a humanitarian.

And she upgraded our seats on the plane without a word. Maybe she's just a generous person.

Owen nudged a ball around with a couple toddlers. The boys giggled and screamed with every pass.

Shyla gathered up a group of little girls. They tossed the underinflated volleyball around as they sang a song reminiscent of "Hot Potato."

Within minutes, the whole town knew about Kat's giveaway. The littlest kids had no hesitation in coming up and seeing what they could get. But some of the older kids were a bit tentative, perhaps silently wondering if they were too old to claim a toy.

One of the boys at the edge of the audience had his eyes fixed on the soccer ball I was inflating next. He looked about eleven. His boyish face had lost its baby fat but didn't quite have manly features yet. He wore a faded green shirt with the Incredible Hulk on it.

I held up the ball. "Hey, Hulk, want this?"

He looked at me skeptically.

"Te gusta Incredible Hulk?" I tried.

The boy understood "Incredible Hulk." He stood up a little prouder and pulled the bottom of his shirt tight with his thumbs. He took a couple steps forward, stopped, and looked around like he expected an adult to usher him away from the toys meant for little kids only.

I tossed him the ball, and in true soccer player fashion, he let it hit his chest as he leaned backward. The ball fell to his feet, and as it hit the ground, he put his right foot on top before it could bounce. A perfect trap.

He smiled. "Gracias."

I smiled back.

The boy swept the ball behind him with his foot, spun 180 degrees, and pushed the ball up the street. His friends ran after him, and seconds later, they were playing soccer in a small rocky field off the main road.

Watching them convinced me to never donate money to a charity again. Instead, I'd donate time; just two days into this medical mission was enough to realize how much more rewarding it was to help a person than write a check.

"Hey, back to work, ball boy," Kat said from behind me.

I turned to find her holding up a beer. The scene was almost a beer commercial, one where a grubby guy sweating in the sun at some task more laborious than pumping up soccer balls is suddenly treated to a beer by a beautiful woman who is somehow far cleaner than her dusty surroundings.

I grabbed the beer and took a sip. "Thanks. I don't usually drink on the job, but I'll make an exception."

"Want a hand?" she offered.

I took another swig. "I got it."

"I have a feeling you like to do things yourself," she said.

"It's a surgeon's nature." I set the beer down and grabbed another ball. There were only a couple left.

She bounced one of the balls in front of her. "Do you like it?"

"Surgery? Yeah, I love working with my hands."

She watched my actions more closely. "Those hands play any instruments?"

"I play the radio," I said.

"Ha." She raised a little toast. "Thanks for letting me tag along with seeing patients. This is a great escape from...everything."

"It is," I said.

Kat laughed. "Someone posted naked pictures of you on the internet, too?"

"Nothing that horrifying."

She shrugged. "They were supposed to be private pictures for my boyfriend. I was stupid to take them."

Did she say "boyfriend"? Well, that sucks.

I genuflected a tiny bit. "On behalf of men worldwide, I'm sorry so many of us are jerks. You seem to be dealing with the cream of the crop." Nearby, Owen caught my eye and winked as he passed the ball with the boys. I looked away and back at Kat.

"It's hard to believe in evolution when natural selection hasn't given women another option," she agreed.

"I think we serve a unique purpose," I offered.

"Only by default. If we could multiply without you, men would be as vestigial as an appendix."

"Vestigial?" I repeated. How did she know that word?

Kat smiled. "I'm not an idiot. I used to love science, especially the human body . . . even the parts that become useless as we evolve."

I straightened and backed up a little. "I didn't say you were an idiot."

She tucked a few hairs behind her ear. "Thanks for showing me that polyp. I know I was rude when we met so I'm partway to blame for starting at zero with you guys. Probably less than zero for Ziggler." She smiled. "But just because I don't work in a hospital doesn't mean I'm worthless. If it weren't for the song that made me famous, I would have been a doctor."

I smiled back. A doctor? I'd have to find out more about that later. "The Ziggler thing isn't personal. I think I started at less than zero with him, too."

"Well, it's great to hear most of the people in Ziggler's world except for Owen are standing knee-deep in shit."

"Knee-deep? Now that's an optimistic way of looking at things," I said.

Kat cocked her head and raised an eyebrow.

"You're in it up to your armpits at least," I said, grinning.

Kat punched me on the shoulder.

For me, being hit by a woman was just as good as being hit *on* by one.

***

After we gave out the last of the balls, Owen ushered us back to the clinic to see a couple of patients before dinner. Patients who needed surgery.

Kat stuck with me, so I had to make it worth her while. I felt the cyst in the upper midline of a female patient's neck. The woman was slender, and the lump above her Adam's apple was about the size of a strawberry. "Here's something almost vestigial for you," I said to Kat.

She looked closer as I explained what we were looking at. "This is a thyroglossal duct cyst. The thyroid gland actually starts up near the tongue and descends to its position during development. In some people, the migratory path remains as a closed tube that fills with fluid years later and creates a cyst. Ask her to look up and swallow."

Kat interpreted, and the patient swallowed, making the cyst bob up and down.

I nodded. "That confirms the diagnosis. When the cyst is attached to the hyoid bone, it moves with the rest of the larynx when she swallows. A skin cyst won't do that."

"Cool," Kat said. "But what's a hyoid bone?"

"The horseshoe-shaped bone in your upper neck that a bunch of muscles attach to. Like this." I made my thumb and index finger into a C-shape, turned it horizontal, and pinched my neck just below my jaw.

Kat grinned. "That's the sort of stuff that first made me want to

66

go to med school. I'm too old now, though."

I frowned at her. "How old are you?"

"Thirty."

I shook my head. "Oh yeah, you're ancient. Probably best you find yourself a retirement home."

She turned serious. "I always wanted to go, but the song happened. I thought I'd take a year off and tour and make money to pay for med school. But the song went international, and so did the touring." She turned away, her head down like she was confessing a sin.

I began examining our patient's cyst again so Kat wouldn't feel so self-conscious. "I think anyone would have done the same. A hit song is a dream come true."

Kat patted our waiting patient's hand. "It was, but it turned out to be a 'be careful what you wish for' scenario. The lifestyle wasn't for me. I thought I could go back to normal, but everything around me had changed, even my friends. Sometimes I think I should start over. Change my name, dye my hair, move somewhere new."

Interesting. "What's your boyfriend think of that?"

"Ex-boyfriend. He's the one who leaked the photos."

Even more interesting.

Owen popped his head into the room. "Are you two done? It's dinner time."

We finished examining the patient and then joined Owen and the others in the dining area, where Sister Torres served us a meal of sausage, beans, rice, and beer. Not much different than the night before.

As soon as Sister Torres left the room, Shyla leaned forward. "Luis's mom told me the Nochedrilo bit her finger off," she said in a hushed voice.

"The kids' monster?" Owen asked.

Shyla nodded. "Because she sinned."

Ziggler snorted in disapproval.

Owen held up his hand. "This is a way-back place, remember. Life here seems even tougher now than it was when I visited years ago.

Religion is how it's been for millennia, the cause and answer for everything. Bad things are punishments for sins. The locals don't see life the same way we do in America."

"But *something* bit off her finger!" Shyla said. "No way am I going into that jungle."

Owen shrugged his shoulders. "It may be a little lie to cover up something more embarrassing. It's much easier to blame it on a monster."

Kat and I exchanged glances. She'd certainly had her share of embarrassing moments . . . and monsters.

Ziggler stood. "There's a monster in everyone's life. I'll see you guys in the morning." He grabbed his beer and walked out of the room with a slight limp, favoring his right leg.

"What's with him?" Kat asked. "He ate fast and didn't say a single word during dinner."

Owen looked at the door Ziggler had just walked through. "Like he said, everyone's got a monster. His is a bitter divorce."

Shyla bit her lip. "I was wondering. He was a lot more fun on our last mission."

Owen took a sip of his beer. "His ex-wife has been using anything and everything as ammo against him. She even got custody of their kids just because he has to go in on call some nights. The guy loves being a doctor, and his ex somehow convinced a judge that's a sin. I think kicking those soccer balls with the boys earlier today reminded him of his kids. I'm hoping this trip will remind him the world's not all bad."

Shyla held up her own beer. "Maybe the world's not all bad, but that Nochedrilo is and he's real."

Chapter 8

After we finished our cases the next afternoon, Owen gave us the option to chill out or take a walk into the jungle. Kat had disappeared into her room, but the rest of us were ready for an adventure.

As we walked down the street, the locals greeted us with friendly smiles. Kids paused from playing with their new balls to wave. Shyla seemed to have reached Kat's level of celebrity status as a group of little girls crowded around to say hi.

Owen clapped Ziggler on the back. "They've accepted us into the tribe. I told you this place was great."

"Anywhere away from lawyers is great," Ziggler said.

"C'mon, man, just admit it. You're having more fun than you thought," Owen said.

Ziggler nodded a tiny bit.

"I saw a smile!" Owen howled as he bounced back and forth behind Ziggler.

Shyla looked at me. "Is this how he is with you?"

"No, I've been wondering why he seems so sedate," I deadpanned.

Ziggler actually cracked a smile.

As we continued our walk, I noticed a vine wrapping around a house that would make a good photo. I reached into my pocket and came up empty. I knew if I ventured into the rainforest without my camera, we'd see a puma wrestling an anaconda while a family of tapirs looked on. "I forgot my camera," I called to the others. "You go ahead and I'll catch up."

"We can wait," Owen offered.

Ziggler turned toward a trailhead at the edge of the road. "I'll keep going since I'm kinda slow as is."

I waved Owen and Shyla on. "Go with him, but if the trail forks, wait for me."

Shyla sighed. "Okay, but if you see Kat, try and get her to come along."

I jogged back into town, a few townsfolk giving me nods and smiles as I went by. There was something quaint to me, even romantic, about what seemed like their quieter, simpler life here. That's why I loved hiking; it was an escape into a world where I felt I belonged. Just me and nature, a little bug crawling on a twig on the tree of life. The same could be said about a city, but in the city I felt like a cog in a machine. In nature, I was free to roam the land, see the world how it was supposed to be, eat a berry here and there, but leave no trace. I relished being the nearly invisible visitor, like a buck glimpsed in the headlights, here and gone.

I turned onto the side street just past the school and spotted a barefoot boy knocking on my door while holding a cloth to his forehead. When he saw me, his face lit up. He was the boy with the Incredible Hulk T-shirt I'd given a soccer ball to the day before.

"Doctor! Doctor!" He ran up to me and stopped, pulling the cloth down from his forehead enough to reveal blood oozing from a deep laceration. The cut was about five centimeters long and down to the muscle. He needed stitches.

Little trails of blood dried on his left temple. Stripes of clean skin marked where his tears had cut trails through the dirt on his face. People never cut themselves in a sterile environment.

"Cual es su nombre?" I asked.

The boy smiled at my funny accent or bad Spanish. He answered, but I didn't catch what he said. It wasn't a common name.

I tried to repeat it back to the boy. "Sinswertay?"

The boy smiled and nodded.

I gave him the stop sign signal with my hand. "Wait a sec," I said as I unlocked the door. Inside, I grabbed my camera, just in case I did catch up with the others. I hoped they wouldn't wait for me. I wished I could have texted them to go ahead but we were back in the days of waiting and wondering.

I also snatched my Rubik's Cube out of my bag. It would be a good distraction for my patient. Chances were the kid had never seen anything like it before.

The boy's eyes were stuck on the multicolored cube before I even exited my room. I motioned for him to follow me to the front of the building. "C'mon, Sinswertay, we need to sew you up."

Inside the front door we ran into Kat. "I thought you went on a hike," she said, putting her hand on her hip like she was a mom waiting for an answer.

I pointed at my injured patient. "I was on my way, but now I've got to sew Sinswertay closed. You want to help?"

Kat's face lit up. "For real?"

"Of course. You're the only one here."

She pouted. "So I'm your last choice?"

"My one and only choice," I said.

She smiled. "You sure do know how to make a girl feel special." She took Sinswertay's free hand and started walking him to the recovery room. She looked back at me. "Sin suerte, huh?"

"I think that's what he said," I replied, starting to wonder.

She looked at the boy. "Sin suerte?"

The boy grinned like he'd been caught in a lie, but nodded yes at the same time.

"What?" I asked, now knowing I'd been had somehow.

Kat grinned, too. "'Sin suerte' means 'bad luck.'"

Ooh, that kid played you. Sucka.

I led them into the empty recovery room. "It fits. That gash across his forehead looks like bad luck to me. Can you ask him where his parents are?"

Kat knelt in front of him, had a brief conversation, and then looked up at me. "Working at the plantation. It's apparently pretty far away."

I couldn't help smiling. I'd been hoping to get away from bureaucracy, and here I was in a town where bureaucracy had been so stripped away that I didn't need parental consent, much less consent forms, to treat my young patient.

While I prepared the supplies I'd need to stitch him up, Sin Suerte stretched out on a cot in the recovery room and Kat cleaned his face with a wet cloth. "He says he hit his head on a table edge playing soccer in his house."

Which pretty much made his injury my fault, thanks to me giving him the ball. I tapped the syringe I was holding upside-down to get the air bubbles to the top. When they collected under the hub I pushed the plunger to squirt them out through the needle until a tiny bit of medicine sprayed out the tip. "Tell him this is going to hurt, but in a minute, it won't."

As Kat translated, the boy nodded as if he understood, but kept his wide eyes on the syringe. Fear flickered across his face and he started squeezing his fingertips in anticipation of the shot. He may have been on the cusp of wanting to be one of the "big kids," but the sight of the needle very much made him a little boy.

"Let him hold your hand," I told Kat.

Kat smiled and offered Sin her hand.

I shook my head. "Actually, only give your first two fingers. A strong person can dislocate a bone when crushing three."

Kat sighed. "They teach you how to hold hands in medical school?"

"Yeah. It's second-year material."

She smiled. "That's why it's four years, huh?"

I gave Sin Suerte a nod to warn him I was starting. I pushed firmly next to my injection site as a distraction and then I inserted the needle into his skin near the cut. He squeezed Kat's fingers and winced out a whimper. A moment later he looked up at me and raised his eyebrows. Was that it?

I smiled and nodded again. "The slower the injection, the less the pain," I told Kat. "The nerves come from above the eyebrow. By injecting the lower part of the wound first, the nerve is numb by the time I get to the upper half."

Kat seemed impressed. "Every move you make is planned."

"Ideally. Surgery isn't supposed to be ad-libbed. It's supposed to be like knitting—rhythmic, planned, and relaxing," I said.

You know she thinks you're talking about masturbating.

"So what do you need me for?" Kat asked.

"Entertainment."

"You want me to tell you a joke or something? Or am I here just to feed your ego?" Her face sank as she said it.

I touched around the periphery of the laceration with the tip of the needle, but Sin didn't flinch. "Not my entertainment, you goofball. *His.* Your sister is a master at distracting a patient with nonstop conversation."

Kat gave me a long blink and tilted her head to the side. "Well, if it's a competition against my big sis, I'm in." She rapped the top of her skull with her knuckles and a hollow sound emanated from her mouth. The little boy laughed. I smiled.

As I washed the wound and then prepped the surrounding skin with iodine, Kat started talking to Sin. I couldn't catch much of what they were saying, but I did hear him say "Nochedrilo." And right after he said it, Kat whipped her head toward me.

"He says his dad works for Nochedrilo," she said.

"What's that mean?" I asked. I stopped sewing while Kat asked Sin a question. Sin looked up at me with a face full of hesitation and worry.

I threw another stitch trying to hide my eagerness to hear Sin's response. "Tell him we're the good guys."

Kat coaxed some more conversation out of Sin. I tried to be patient, but it wasn't in my nature. I watched his face for clues, there were hints of surprise and disbelief, but mostly he looked scared, more scared of Nochedrilo than the needle I had just poked him with.

Finally, Kat turned back toward me. "He says Nochedrilo runs a cocaine plantation for something called the Shining Path. But here the farmers are called *cocaleros*. It's not a word I know."

I thought of the men loading into the truck that morning. "What's this Nochedrilo look like?"

Kat asked our patient and then translated back to me. "He's a short man, he always wears black, and he has a tattoo of a crocodile on his arm."

Probably the badass who punched the worker.

"Y él come dedos," Sin said.

Kat curled her upper lip in disgust. "And he eats fingers."

What the fuck?

The doctor was missing parts of his fingers. So was the mom of the kid with giant tonsils. She'd said the Nochedrilo had eaten them.

I could imagine Nochedrilo biting off the doctor's fingers. What a dick.

Sin looked up at me—curious, no longer entertained.

"Have him try the Rubik's cube," I said as I started sewing again. Anything to break the strange tension.

Kat picked up the cube and mixed up with a dozen quick twists. Sin Suerte watched with curiosity. Kat handed it to him. He glanced up at me for permission to move his hands, which I granted with a nod.

Sin gave the cube a few turns, slowly and hesitantly, just to see how it worked. Then he started to get all the red stickers on the same side. After five minutes, he handed it back to Kat, slightly frustrated. "Resolverlo," he said to her.

"Tell him I'll solve it in a few minutes. I'm almost done," I said.

But Kat didn't translate. Instead, she started twisting the cube with a piano-playing type of rhythm. I threw another stitch but then paused to watch Kat's slender fingers work the cube effortlessly. Block after block slid into place. Before long, she'd solved the green side.

"Nice," I said.

The left corner of her mouth crept upward. "Anyone can solve one side." She flipped the cube upside down and started solving the opposite side.

A fire lit inside my chest as my competitive side came to life. I started sewing faster. The race was on.

Is this how nerds flirt? You are such a dork!

I didn't dare look over at her while I threw the last couple stitches, but I could hear the sliding of the cube pick up pace. I tied the knot, cut the tail with the scissors, and finally looked up. "Done."

Kat held the solved cube in the air in front of Sin. He beamed at it, oblivious to both his freshly closed wound and me.

I looked at Kat and smiled. I like brains. In general, and in women.

She smiled back. Her entire face radiated. It was her first real smile of the trip, and it was beautiful.

Chapter 9

Less than half an hour later, Kat and I were at the edge of town and down the path the others had left on. It was about five feet wide in this area, and heavily used.

"You closed that wound perfectly," Kat said.

"Thanks. One of my mentors once told me, 'Close every wound like it's on your mother's face.'"

"Good advice." Kat smiled. "Do you try to do everything perfectly?"

"My dad always said, 'If you're going to do something, do it right.'"

Kat kicked a large stone off the path and into the brush. "I guess so, but don't you worry about becoming a control freak?"

"I don't think so. Freaky stuff happens when no one's in control. Besides, I only control myself. Everyone else is free to do whatever they want."

"Yeah. Did your dad tell you to limit yourself to only one drink?"

I stopped walking. I rarely mentioned my dad to anyone. He was a ghost of the distant pass, but his bits of advice lived on. I looked Kat straight in the eyes and repeated another of his mantras. "Every moment in life is a choice. Just try to make choices you won't regret."

"Does that mean you turn into a raging asshole if you get tipsy?" Kat asked.

I held a leaf back for her. "Don't know. I've never been drunk."

Whoa, numbnuts. You don't say that to others, even if it's true.

Kat looked at me sideways as she stepped over a tree root. "Wow, you're a lot more serious than anyone else I know."

"I don't think you really know me. One of my guiding principles is to have fun."

"Calculated fun." Kat went monotone. "Hooray." She emphasized each syllable of the word with a pump of her fist.

I shrugged and let her teasing go. Did uncalculated fun mean alcohol and drugs? What was wrong with not wanting to get drunk? I liked being me; I had no desire to escape myself or my grasp of reality.

We caught up to the others in only fifteen minutes. They'd waited for me awhile, and Shyla had talked with some locals. Turns out a lot of them bathe in the river, so Shyla had learned we needed to take the fork on the left if we wanted to avoid an embarrassing scene.

The group moved at a snail's pace, which was just fine with me; I liked looking at the underside of large leaves for insects or waiting near a tree to see what bird was making noise.

"Hey, you guys," I called. The group stopped and turned to watch me push over an old log. His hiding spot was revealed, a large black beetle scampered under some leaves instead.

Shyla ducked behind Ziggler and pointed at the giant reddish-brown centipede with yellow legs sitting in the hollowed-out dirt where the log had been. "Oh my God, oh my God."

"Wow, look at that thing," Ziggler said. "I bet it's six inches long."

Owen chuckled. "Unzip your fly, Ziggler. If it's twice as long as your wanger, we'll know it's six inches."

Kat let out a little "Ugh."

Shyla gave Owen a slight whack to the back of his shoulder. "Owen, *please!* I swear, you're worse than my twelve-year-old."

I picked up the longest stick I could find and poked the centipede with it. The bug shot forward with unexpected speed. We all whooped and shrieked.

"That does it," Shyla said. "Now I'll sit up all night with the light on."

We kept moving along the trail. Less than a minute later, a loud screech came from overhead. I scanned the sky, expecting to see a pterodactyl swooping down on us.

"What was that?" Kat asked.

"A black crocodile about to jump out of the trees onto you," Owen said.

Just overhead, between gaps in the canopy, a handful of blue-and-yellow birds flew overhead in tight formation. The birds seemed almost prehistoric in size, their wingspans stretching two and a half feet.

"Wow," Kat said.

"Macaws," Ziggler told us. "They're pretty common around here. My aunt used to have one as a pet."

I felt something prickly on the back of my neck. Something with barbed feet. And it was big, at least a few inches.

Dude, there's something crawling on you! Maybe it's that big, ugly centipede. Is it a wandering spider? It better not be a spider.

I imagined a big, black, hairy spider meandering slowly toward my hairline. Goosebumps tore across my body. Some giant poisonous spider was probably just looking for the best bite to take.

Think positively. It could be a hairless spider. Those are the safe ones, right?

"Um, you guys." I tried not to move a muscle as I said it.

The fear in my voice got everyone's attention. They turned in unison like choreographed dancers.

"What is it?" Owen asked. He scanned the area. "Is it a snake? A scorpion?" He threw out guesses as if I had started a game of scary invertebrate charades.

I slowly turned away from them. "It's on the back of my neck."

Shyla stepped back quickly. "Oh my God, oh my God. Oh...huh."

Kat stepped closer. "Here, hand me your camera."

I shivered as I gave her my camera. "How about telling me what it is?"

Owen leaned in. "It's fantastic. It's a giant praying mantis."

"Yeah, she thinks she's bringing you home for dinner," Ziggler said.

I reached back to pull her off my neck, and the mantis ran onto the top of my head. The camera clicked. I swept the mantis into my hand, and she leaned onto her back four legs, holding her front two up in her namesake position. Her triangular head looked like it belonged on a sketch of the alien found at Roswell.

Kat snapped a few more shots.

"Aren't you scared?" Shyla asked.

"They're harmless," I said. "When I was a kid, finding a mantis like this would have been a dream come true. This thing's huge."

"Who dreams about mantises?" Kat asked.

"Nerds," Owen answered.

Shyla slapped Owen on the back.

Owen laughed. "I'm sorry, he was just a kid. Nerdlets."

I set the mantis down, thanking her silently for honoring me with a visit.

Okay, I agree, life is amazing . . . even that little long-armed, husband-killing critter.

We walked for a minute in silence before Kat spoke up. "You guys are lucky to be a group of friends that can work and travel together," she said. "I wish I had something like that."

"You're rich and famous. If you aren't happy, the rest of us poor saps don't stand a chance," Ziggler said.

"There's a lot more to happiness than fame and money," Kat said.

"Not to most people," Ziggler grumbled.

"What's making you unhappy?" I asked Kat. It fascinated me when people knew exactly what was wrong but didn't fix it.

"I don't like being famous," Kat started. "Don't get me wrong. It was awesome at the beginning. Not so much the fame aspect, but knowing I created something so many people loved." She paused, picking at her fingernails absently. I wanted to hear the thoughts she wasn't saying.

"It was incredibly uplifting to have random people smile at me, thank me, or cheer me on," she continued. "If everyone was always like that—cheering on the random person, waving, smiling—the world would be a better place."

Shyla remained quiet. A sparkle in her eye hinted she was happy just to hear her sister talk. Shyla might be Kat's biggest fan. Did Kat know it?

"I'm serious. You guys must know what I'm talking about. Doesn't it feel good to know you've made people better?"

"Yeah, but people aren't asking for my autograph," Ziggler said.

"What about you, Rees?" Kat asked.

"Sure. One time, I was walking to my car in the grocery store parking lot and a girl driving by hollered out the window, 'Thanks for taking out my tonsils.' That was pretty cool. But for the most part, the satisfaction comes from the inside. Just knowing I did what I could for someone is fulfilling in itself."

"Exactly. That's why we're all here," Owen said. "It's not because we couldn't find another way to spend our vacations. You've got a level three problem."

Kat stopped, "Level three?"

Owen stopped beside her. "I promise I won't be too preachy."

The rest of us stopped, too, as Owen continued. "Level one is basic survival . . . food, water, shelter. Level two is wants and comforts, like a car, or a spouse, a career, things that bring convenience and happiness to achieving level one. The third level is one most people don't think about, at least not outside their own family. It is what you do to make the world better. It's helping others. It's what you've done in the third level that lives on long after you die, and it's what gives you the satisfaction Rees was talking about. We save one life here and we get nothing for it except satisfaction. We go home and that person lives, has a family of their own. Now our actions trickle through generations."

We all stayed quiet a moment.

Kat bit her lower lip. "I'm caught up in doing things that aren't fulfilling with people who aren't even my friends."

"Isn't that most of life?" Ziggler asked.

"That's why we're here, to remind you that it's not," Owen said.

I admired Owen. I never would have guessed that under all his silly jokes he harbored such strong feelings on how to make life more gratifying.

It all fits. Micro-penis jokes are the stepping-stones to fulfillment. Doesn't most philosophy boil down to knowing when to laugh?

"Is that rain?" Shyla asked.

Before we could look up, the clouds let loose heavy raindrops. We let out a chorus of groans and wails. As the others scampered ahead, I stayed back with Ziggler. Maybe I could find what made him tick.

"Why did Owen call you sheep-hearted?" I asked.

"He's just being a goofy. You know Owen," he said.

"Is that the opposite of lion-hearted?" I asked.

"It's nothing," he said firmly.

End of conversation.

***

That night's dinner was not the much-anticipated guinea pig. There were some awesome yucca fries and a thick stew with a variety of vegetables, though. We started out with business—the next day's cases.

The next morning we were scheduled to remove a giant thyroid. Shyla would scrub in to lend an extra hand. But tomorrow's cases weren't what was on my mind . . . or Kat's.

As soon as the planning was over, Kat jumped in. "What are we going to do about Dr. Yanpa?"

Ziggler rolled his head back, but I didn't think Kat was being dramatic. We didn't know what Yanpa was capable of.

"I told you, nothing," Owen said. "It's an idle threat. If he comes back, we'll give him a hundred bucks and tell him to scram."

"But what if he isn't an idle threat? There are bad people around here," Shyla said. By now everyone had heard what Kat and I learned from Sin Suerte.

"The guy's a doctor, not a cocaine grower," Owen asked. "He can't be *that* bad."

Shyla, Kat, and I looked at Owen for a better answer. There seemed to be no limit to how bad people could be. The guy was extorting us; he was *that* bad.

Owen sank back in his chair. "Okay, we have two more days... plenty of time," he said. "Last time I was here, we didn't pay any bribes, but I don't remember meeting Dr. Yanpa back then. I'll talk to Sister Torres and ask her how other medical teams handled him."

Shyla relaxed her posture, and Owen continued, "I'll give that unethical piece of shit two grand over my dead body."

I like Owen. He's got balls. If you were in charge, you'd be scrambling together two large.

"I don't know. There's a guy here who bites people's fingers off and a doc extorting us for all that he can," I said. Suddenly hospital administrators didn't seem so bad.

"The same thing happened to me in Kenya." Owen said. "Like it or not, these places do have routines, and the shakedown is part of it. I'm not saying it's right or okay, it's just how they do things. We're here to administer medicine, not the law."

"Maybe a little law enforcement would make it easier for us to be doctors," I said.

"Just let me try it my way first," Owen said.

Which was exactly how he'd approached Mrs. Childs' airway back home, right before convincing me to come on this mission. If anything, Owen was consistent.

I didn't like it.

Chapter 10

Ziggler's patient had a goiter that nearly touched her chin. The skin on the right side of her neck bulged like it was stretched over a cantaloupe. I doubted she was capable of looking at her feet without bending at the back.

Despite the goiter's giant size, the anatomy wasn't any different. Just tie off the feeding vessels, separate the gland's attachment to the trachea, and leave behind the important stuff. The only problem was getting exposure.

Ziggler started the surgery while I assisted with Sister Torres. We quickly realized we needed a fourth set of hands to retract the muscles overlying the gland while Ziggler and I detached it from its feeding vessels.

Ziggler's surgical mask didn't stifle his quiet moan. "Where's Shyla?"

"She's got the runs. Kat can help." The way Owen said it, he made it sound like the best thing ever, like we were all going to get ice cream cones. Two scoops!

Kat's mask couldn't hide her excitement. Her wide eyes peered past us at the surgical field.

"What do I do?" she asked.

"Exactly what we say," I told her. "Sister Torres will walk you through getting gowned after you scrub." Sister Torres nodded.

"She can't scrub," Ziggler protested. "She's never done it before."

I gave him a mild glare. "Why not? All she's going to do is hold hook."

Owen didn't give Ziggler time for a rebuttal. "C'mon, Kat. I'll show you how to wash your hands." He pulled her out of the room to the sink to scrub.

As soon as the door closed, Ziggler grunted to me, "Once she's scrubbed, you're responsible for her."

Kat came in a few minutes later holding her dripping hands up in the air. Ziggler stopped operating to watch her like he would pounce at any second. *Underneath that gruff exterior is a solidly gruff man*, I thought.

But Kat didn't give him the satisfaction of screwing up. She did exactly as she was told. She dried one hand with half the towel and then dried the other hand with the other half. Owen mimed every action for her, and soon she was fully gowned and gloved.

"The sterile field is the level of the patient," I said. "If something falls, let it fall. If your forehead itches, have Owen scratch it. If you aren't holding an instrument, hold your hands here." I linked my fingers together like I was praying and set them on the sterile drape covering the patient's shoulder.

"Okay, let's go," Ziggler interrupted.

Kat glanced at him and immediately dismissed his intrusion.

"Here, hold this." I placed a retractor at the top part of the incision on my side of the patient. The retractor looked like a miniature garden hoe fabricated from a single piece of steel. The business end of the retractor was holding back the muscles so we could get to the gland.

Kat took the retractor from my hand. The exposure narrowed.

"Don't be afraid to pull." I put my hand on top of hers and gave it a tug away from the patient. "This is the part where you act like you're waterskiing. Lean back and let your arms really pull on the retractors. It keeps the wound open as wide as it can go and keeps you out of the way."

When I looked at Kat to confirm she understood, her eyes pulled me in. A hat covered her forehead and hair and a surgical mask hid the rest of her face, but all it took was her dark eyes to make her beautiful. They sparkled with lights of their own. Excitement, interest . . . she looked genuinely thrilled to be part of the case.

Hey, Puppy Love. Yeah you, numbnuts. You still have your hand on hers.

I yanked my hand away. "This is one of the most important parts. The superior pole—the top end of the gland—has some large arteries. If one of them gets away from us, it will be a mess." The words rushed out of me. Had she noticed my hand on hers for too long?

Kat pulled hard and I pushed the gland down, making space for Ziggler to reach in with a clamp to get to the blood vessels.

"Back in the day," I explained, "the thyroid was a no-man's-land. Too risky, too bloody. The superior pole can be tricky even with modern techniques, especially in big thyroids. It's hard to see around the bulge of the gland, and there isn't much room for instruments. Still, every blood vessel needs to be double clamped, cut between the clamps, and then tied off with suture."

Kat gave a polite "Hmm" and peered into the wound. Yet again, cherry blossoms.

Sister Torres pushed scissors into my right hand to cut the suture Ziggler was tying.

"How big is the gland supposed to be?" Kat asked.

"Each side is supposed to be about the same size as your thumb," I answered.

"Wow, this one is huge!" Kat said.

Owen cleared his throat. "That's the first time a woman has ever said *that* to Rees."

Fiery embarrassment flowed into my face. I prayed my mask, glasses, and hat shrouded my glowing red skin. Kat herself was a shade pinker than usual, but smiling under her mask. I returned my focus to the surgical field, wishing I could crawl in and hide behind the thyroid.

Ziggler ignored Owen's bad joke and grunted, "Yeah, that's why we're taking it out."

"I've got a good view of this vessel. Mosquito." I reached my hand out.

Sister Torres slapped the narrow clamp into my hand. With a few spreads, I isolated a juicy artery and put a clamp on it. In a few more moves, Ziggler and I had divided it and tied it off.

"What are you doing?" Kat asked.

"We just double clamped and cut one of the main arteries to the thyroid gland. Now I'm going to tie a silk suture around the two ends to prevent a massive mess," I answered.

"Would she die if that tie came off?" Kat asked.

"If it comes off right now, we could stop it. But if it comes off a couple days from now in the middle of the night, it wouldn't be good. As the blood accumulates in the space where her thyroid was, it could pinch her airway shut." I knew more than I wanted to about that situation thanks to Mrs. Childs back home.

"What about her carotid? If that got cut, would she die?" Kat asked.

As I finished tying the vessel, Kat leaned into me to try to get a better look into the wound. Her body pressed hard against my left side.

"We don't just slip and cut carotids," Ziggler said.

Kat leaned in even closer and pointed with her gloved finger. "Wow, that's her airway?"

I thought I could feel her right breast pushing against the side of my left arm. I didn't dare look. My body radiated heat.

Lou, where are you? Don't you have some cutting remark or bad joke?

I'm enjoying this. Watching you lose focus is fun. The iceman is melting. Oh wait, not completely. Looks like part of you is freezing solid.

No.

I think so.

No.

A little.

I cleared my throat. "As soon as we get a couple more vessels free,

I'll give you a tour of the anatomy."

I looked at Sister Torres and then Ziggler. Neither of them seemed to notice that time had stopped moving save for the bead of sweat dripping down my temple.

"You're a pretty good teacher underneath all that surgeon," Kat said.

You've got some moves you can teach her.

I shifted my position, acting like I was getting a better view. The move pushed Kat off. My muscles and mind relaxed.

"Kat, cut the chatter," Ziggler snapped.

Kat straightened and looked Ziggler straight in the eye. "Why don't you like me?"

The whole room screeched to a halt. Owen even stopped bagging the patient for a couple breaths.

Ziggler paused. "I didn't say I didn't like you."

Kat laughed. "I didn't say you *said* it."

As soon as she said that, there was no doubt I really did like her. I respect spunk. Time to change the subject, though. "Let's discuss this later," I told them. "Sister Torres, what can you tell us about Dr. Yanpa?"

Owen gave me a look of disappointment. I'd just stolen his job.

"Dr. Yanpa is a bad man. He thinks people should bow to him. But he is king of nothing."

"That shitball is all talk," Owen said.

"What about this Nochedrilo guy?" Kat asked.

"We don't talk about him," Sister Torres snapped. It was easier to get out a kid's tonsils than to extract information from her. "And don't talk to the villagers about him. The less you mention his name, the better."

Sister Torres grabbed a clamp and slapped it into my hand. She was done talking.

But now I really wanted answers.

Chapter 11

Owen and I closed up the OR for the evening before checking on the woman whose giant thyroid we'd removed. She was going to spend the night in the recovery room with her family. Like most people only a few hours after surgery, she seemed perfectly fine. Not enough time had passed for real inflammation to set in, but she'd be sore in a day or two. For now, she was all smiles and thank-yous.

"You're right," I told Owen as we stepped out into the hall. "It's nice to do medicine without all the hurdles."

Owen clapped once. "I told you, just you and the patients. No C-students. Now let's get some grub."

Dinner was short and quiet without Shyla, whose stomach wasn't ready for real food yet. When Ziggler retired early, Owen got up to go check on Shyla with a sly look that made me think he was leaving me alone with Kat on purpose.

Kat grabbed a lemon-lime soda out of the fridge and handed it to Owen to bring to Shyla. When she returned to the table, she sat in the chair next to me instead of her usual one across the table. "Is this trip what you thought it'd be?"

"I guess so," I said. "Except maybe you." This made her smile. "What about you?" I asked.

She played with a fork left behind on the table. "I was so focused on getting away, I honestly hadn't thought much about where I was going. But that bribe from Dr. Yanpa shocks me more than anything else I've seen here."

I turned so we were sitting knee to knee. "I have no idea what we should do about that. My medical training's molded me into one of those star-shaped screwdrivers. Totally useless in all situations except when a star-shaped screwdriver is exactly what's needed."

Kat leaned forward. "I don't think dealing with Peruvian extortionists is part of anyone's training. Anyway, I've seen enough of you in action to see why my sis thinks you're great."

Really?

Kat took my hand, and I looked down at ours together. Her hands were perfect. Slender fingers, soft skin. Far too delicate for this jungle town.

My eyes caught hers, and Kat didn't look away. "Shyla says you always do the right thing." she said.

Did she just glance at your lips?

"I try," I said. My voice sounded quiet and far away.

Kat leaned closer. "We're doing the right thing,"

"I . . ." I started, then Kat planted her lips on mine. At first it was a gentle kiss that barely made contact, immediately followed by a second longer, firmer kiss. Her hands squeezed mine tightly and I held hers in return.

With my eyes closed, the faint smell of cherry blossoms, and her lips on mine, I felt I was in another world, someplace beautiful, someplace far away from this sticky jungle.

A creaking door ripped me back into reality, and Kat pulled back as Sister Torres rushed into the room. "Rees, there is a sick baby at the door. Can you see her?"

I leapt out of my chair and looked back at Kat. "That was a good-luck kiss," she whispered. Then, in a voice loud enough for Sister Torres to hear, she added, "Let's see what we can do," as we followed the nun out to the street.

We walked out to find a grim-faced couple standing in front of an old black pickup truck, holding a sick child in a painting-perfect moment. Peruvian Gothic. Deep creases radiated from the man's eyes as if he'd spent his whole life squinting into the sun. His black leather boots shone like they'd just come out of the box. His black leather jacket and his dark blue jeans were more worn but clean, and a well-used leather sheath held a knife to his hip. Standard jungle issue.

The woman looked to be in her twenties and didn't have any of the man's ruggedness. She could have been his wife or daughter. Her smooth face was full of worry but still pure with innocent youth. She held her baby toward me without a word. She forces a weak, pleading smile, but her brow stayed low. The baby was very small, maybe four to six months old and wrapped in a red blanket.

I wanted to know what was wrong with the baby, but at the same time I couldn't help notice the truck. With its curves and round headlights, it looked like a collector's item from the 1950s or '60s. Just like the trucks I'd seen picking up the workers before dawn.

But that thought had to wait while I examined the baby. It only takes a second to determine when a patient is truly in distress, and this baby was. Even with a blanket covering most of her body, I could tell she was laboring to breathe, inhaling only a shallow breath every few seconds. There were no sounds of her struggling to get air, so the problem wasn't a blockage in the throat or above. Her pattern of rapid breathing indicated something in her lungs, maybe pneumonia, maybe something weird. I didn't know what sort of diseases babies in the Amazon caught. She seemed too young to have been immunized already, even if vaccines were available.

"Get Owen," I told Kat, and she ran back inside.

The man in black looked at me. "Por favor," he said.

Sister Torres's pale face twisted in fear that seemed beyond worry for the baby. "Please, help him."

I reached for the baby, and the mom handed her to me as the man nodded in approval.

Owen met me just inside the door. "We've got to get this kid some oxygen," I told him as he looked down at her. His eyes met mine and his face said, "Fuck" without him needing to say a word.

He turned to Sister Torres. "Tell them to follow us. Their baby is very sick and needs medicine and oxygen."

Together we rushed to the OR, the parents and Kat close behind. "Any ideas?" I asked Owen softly.

He leaned in so the others couldn't overhear. "We can give her some oxygen, start an IV, and fill her tank with saline and antibiotics. Maybe that's all she needs."

The plan sounded reasonable enough, so Owen had the mother lay the baby on the operating room table while Sister Torres translated that the baby, Jimena, was six months old. She looked scrawny, but it was impossible to tell if she was just a skinny baby, or if she'd burned up her baby fat fighting whatever was making her sick.

Sister Torres continued translating. "She hasn't been eating well the past week, but has only been struggling to breathe the past day."

Other than the rapid rising and falling of Jimena's chest as she took a quick breath every few seconds, she seemed listless. Normally babies will arouse when poked and at least look around, but Jimena didn't care when Owen put a pulse oximeter on her finger.

The pulse ox measured her heart rate and blood oxygenation, and quickly told us her heart was racing at 180 beats per minute. An active young man might have a heart rate in the sixties, and healthy babies around 120 beats per minute. 180 was too fast. Her temperature was 102.1, a real fever. Her oxygenation level was 81 percent, not good. It should have been 100 percent, or at least in the high nineties.

This jungle makes half the world's oxygen and this poor girl can't get a good breath . . .

Sister Torres couldn't find a blood pressure cuff small enough for Jimena, and Owen couldn't find a decent vein on her, either. After trying her arms and legs, he looked at her scalp, which can be a good access point on babies. No luck.

But there was one more option, more commonly used in children than adults: intraosseous (I-O) access. By putting a needle directly into the bone marrow of the tibia, the medicine and IV fluid is rapidly taken up into the blood stream. In essence, bone marrow is a non-collapsible vein.

Owen asked Sister Torres to tell Jimena's parents to look away while he inserted the needle. The last thing we needed was Dad (it's more often Dad than Mom) passing out while watching a needle go into his daughter's leg.

"What do you need me to do?" I asked.

Owen threaded a skinny spinal needle into a much larger needle. "Just help hold her still."

Kat stepped up next to me at the side of the OR table. "I can help, too."

"What are you doing?" I asked Owen.

"We don't have an I-O kit," he replied. "If I use just the 16-gauge, I'm afraid a bit of bone will clog the shaft. I'm hoping this other needle will block the hole enough, or at least let me push out the tiny bit of bone that gets into the tip."

I-O kit needles have a solid metal insert, an introducer, within the shaft. The introducer provides strength to the hollow shaft of the needle, and prevents a chunk of tissue from clogging the needle. Owen's improvisation was the best we could hope for without a kit.

I shook my head in admiration. "Didn't know you could do that."

Owen looked at me, face flat. "Me neither."

Real medicine isn't algorithms; it's trying what isn't in the book to help the patient when you have no other options. Owen didn't have a bead of sweat on him. He was ready to try whatever it took.

As he wiped an alcohol pad across Jimena's leg and then grasped it firmly, I put one hand on her hip and the other on her other leg. Her skin felt unnaturally warm. My gut said Jimena wasn't going to live.

I hate it when your gut talks. That fucker is almost always right.

With one firm motion, Owen plunged the needle through the skin of Jimena's lower leg. The needle paused as it hit the bone and with a palpable pop, broke through the cortex into the marrow.

It should have hurt, but Jimena hardly moved as she let out only the tiniest of cries.

Owen wiggled the inner needle back and forth. It seemed to move easily. Not jammed closed with bone. He raised his eyebrows at me, obviously a little surprised his improvisation had worked. A moment later, he had the needle secured with tape and IV fluid dripping into her tibia.

He nodded with satisfaction. "As soon as she perks up enough, I'll start a real IV and get that out of there."

"Nice job, gentlemen," Sister Torres said as she turned the parents around. I didn't deserve any credit, though. I hadn't been more than a cheerleader for Owen, but saying it out loud would have opened the door to bad jokes. This wasn't the time for joking. We were only rehydrating Jimena, not actually curing any disease.

Sister Torres pulled chairs close to the bed so Jimena's parents could sit. When her father hung his jacket on the back of one of the chairs, I spotted a large black tattoo decorating his right forearm.

A black crocodile.

Shit!

I looked at Sister Torres, who gave me a subtle nod with not-so-subtle fear in her eyes. Now I understood her earlier reaction. It wasn't Jimena's illness she'd been terrified by, but Jimena's father.

Your mom would flip if she knew you were treating a drug warlord's daughter. "Hey, Mom, I went to Peru to help get the sick cocaleros back to health."

I had to tell Owen, but when I looked over at him, he was already looking at me. He knew. Kat, too, had her eyes fixed on the crocodile tattoo. The reptile pulsed with every muscle twitch of the man's arm.

Owen turned to her slowly, trying to keep his voice light. "Kat, I don't think we'll need your help from here. But before you go to bed, let Ziggler know what's going on, okay?"

Kat bit her lower lip and nodded in agreement. "Good luck," she said, giving me a worried look while maintaining eye contact as long as possible before she left the room.

Jimena perked up a little as her body rehydrated from the IV. Her heart rate lowered, but her oxygen level stayed low and her respirations high. Through the stethoscope, I heard her lungs crackle like Velcro separating with every breath.

Sister Torres let the parents take a listen to first Jimena's lungs and then their own. She tried to explain the crackles meant spaces that were supposed to be filled with air were filled with fluid instead.

Owen talked to me under his breath while they were distracted. "Her oxygenation isn't improving. I think we should intubate her."

He looked at me for approval, but I frowned. "We aren't equipped for it. This kid needs an ICU, a workup, the right meds, and a whole team of people to care for her."

Owen tilted his head toward Jimena's parents. "You going to tell them that?"

I shook my head. "We don't even have a ventilator."

"We'll just take turns bagging her."

I looked down at our tiny patient. "For how long? Hours? Days?" If we knew we had the right treatment, the right disease, it would at

92

least establish a timeline. But this was just a shot in the dark. No guarantees. No real plan. No nothing.

Owen looked straight at me. "I can't be the guy that didn't try. This is that third level I was talking about. We save her life, and she lives to be someone's grandmother. It's why we're here. Without us, she'll die before she gets to Tarapoto."

"I know, I know," I said. "But if someone comes through the front door with a ruptured aorta, I'm not going to crack his chest and try to sew it shut. She's critical, and we don't have the luxuries of our hospital back home. I'm saying we shouldn't try to battle futility in the back of a church in the Amazon."

Owen put his head in his hands. "Okay, okay. Let me think. I'm not necessarily agreeing with you, but we don't have to decide this minute. She's stable enough to wait."

I felt certain Owen would realize our limitations once he thought this situation through. If we intubated Jimena, she'd have to stay intubated at least two days. That's just how it went with babies. That meant at least two days of IV meds and constant monitoring.

Sister Torres came around the bed to join us. "If she's stable enough, why don't you two go get something to drink and discuss a plan? I'll stay here with them. I can squeeze the bag. They know the routine."

It was a generous offer. We could talk more frankly in private. And then it hit me; Sister said *they know the routine*. Dr. Yanpa's same words, and a not so subtle bit of guidance...

"No need," Owen said.

...That Owen missed altogether.

We might be prolonging the checkmate in a game against Death if we intubated Jimena. I thought about Dr. Yanpa. The jerk had said to let the routine be the routine. But maybe he was right in this sort of case? What sort of routine would Jimena have gone through if we hadn't been here? What sort of routine was Nochedrilo expecting? Where was an ambulance and a major medical center with a pediatric intensive care unit when you needed it?

The pulse oximeter alarmed. Jimena's oxygen level had dropped.

Owen grabbed the laryngoscope and put it into her mouth. Routine or not, he was ready to intubate.

Jimena's parents recoiled in terror. Sister Torres tried comforting them, but it wasn't working as their faces twisted in horror at the sight of the metal instrument being inserted into their baby's mouth.

Owen and I had seen patients intubated thousands of times. But these parents, they'd probably never even seen the procedure reenacted on television. Jimena's mother covered the lower half of her face with her hand as Nochedrilo cried out and waved his hands in protest, the crocodile on his muscular arm bulging forward like it was about to strike.

Owen threaded the clear plastic endotracheal tube into Jimena's airway. A second later, he attached a bag to the end of the endotracheal tube. One end of the bag was connected to an oxygen line, the other the tube. Owen squeezed the bag, forcing air through the tube into the baby's lungs. Her chest rose as her lungs filled with air.

It wouldn't take much imagination to believe that Owen had just created some macabre inflatable toy out of Jimena. Every squeeze of Owen's hand expanded the girl's chest, driving home the perception that she was no longer breathing for herself.

As Sister Torres kept explaining what was happening, the parents looked more and more skeptical. It takes incredible effort and faith to let a doctor be a doctor, and Nochedrilo didn't look like a man of faith. He looked more like he wanted to pull out his knife and stab Owen.

The mother turned away and buried her head into Nochedrilo's shoulder. Then she looked back, a few tears breaking free from the corners of her eyes. Nochedrilo put one arm around his wife and squeezed the edge of the bed with his other hand.

Owen focused his attention on his monitors, seemingly oblivious to the parents' shock. "She's doing great," he said to no one and everyone. "Her heart rate's slowed some and she's getting oxygen."

While Sister Torres interpreted his good news, Owen gave me an "I told you so" glance. I wanted to tell him I'd never doubted his medical decision to intubate her. What I doubted was whether it was feasible. But that didn't matter now; Owen had done exactly what he'd wanted. Now Jimena just needed to survive. Until then, the crocodile on Nochedrilo's arm wasn't going to relax.

When Ziggler arrived to check on us and offer help a few minutes later, Owen sent him away. Before he left, though, Ziggler sized up Nochedrilo. He looked at us and said he'd be back in a few hours to give us a break, sooner if we needed him.

I was too concerned about Jimena to worry about Nochedrilo posing any danger to us. He and Sister Torres exchanged rapid-fire conversation as Owen and I worked. There was an intensity to their words, but I wouldn't say they were arguing. Though I was happy Shyla and Kat weren't in the room, part of me still wished they were there to interpret for me. I was hoping Sister Torres was explaining that intubation was a means to deliver more oxygen to Jimena's lungs, but wasn't in itself a cure.

I sat and bagged Jimena for an hour so Owen could get some rest. She was mostly swaddled in white blankets, but I could still watch her chest rise with every breath delivered through the tube. Her parents, Sister Torres, and I all stared at her expectantly, as if any moment she'd flash us a sign that she was improving. The monitor beeped with every heartbeat, a consistent 164 beats per minute. If her heartbeat was a song, it would be far more up-tempo than the moment called for.

I wanted to know what we were up against. Which disease were we dealing with? Why? Without answers or direction, we were trying to whack a piñata while blindfolded and swinging a drinking straw instead of a bat.

But here was Jimena with a plastic tube sticking out of her mouth and taped to her chin. Fragile, tiny, hardly alive long enough to warrant being killed by some unseen disease.

Hey, buddy, you just defined the word "tragedy." If people could foresee and fix everything, then the word wouldn't exist.

Sister Torres excused herself for a break, and I tried my pidgin Spanish on Jimena's parents by asking their names.

"Evelyn y Diego," Nochedrilo replied. No surprise he didn't tell me his true identity.

I looked at Evelyn, whose gaze hadn't moved from her baby's face, or her hand from her baby's foot. "Sólo niña?" I asked.

Evelyn nodded. "Sobrevivira?"

"Sí," I said, but then I wondered if she'd meant, "Is she alive?" or "Will she live?" All I was sure of was that vivo meant live.

I waited for Sister Torres to return before I said anything else. Once she was back, though, I found I didn't have much to say.

Owen came back from his brief nap and checked the monitors. He massaged his brow with his thumb and index finger, and I realized this was the first time I'd ever seen him nervous.

He looked over at me. "It is what it is, my friend. It's up to Mother Nature now."

"It's always up to Mother Nature. She decides who wins." I said. Doctors and patients alike fool themselves into thinking otherwise.

Mother Nature announced her arrival about ten minutes later, when Jimena's heart rate and oxygen fell. Then she flatlined.

I started giving her chest compressions. It doesn't take much effort to compress a baby's chest. Adult's rib cages are less flexible because the cartilage attachments turn to bone as we get older.

Evelyn threw herself onto the bottom part of the OR table and wailed.

I didn't stop the CPR.

Sister Torres put an arm around Evelyn, eventually prying her off the table and hurrying her out the door. But Nochedrilo ignored her urging to follow, waving Sister Torres off like a bothersome fly. He didn't say a word, just clenched his jaw and stared through slit eyelids as we tried to resuscitate his daughter.

I pumped on Jimena's chest at 120 beats per minute. Push in, relax, let her chest spring back out, push in. Years before, a CPR instructor had told me that "I Will Survive" is the rhythm to follow for infant CPR, while "Stayin' Alive" was best for adults. In my head, Gloria Gaynor's voice sang to me over and over that she was afraid, then petrified.

So was I.

Owen puffed breaths into Jimena's endotracheal tube. Her pulse oximeter was no longer working, but the dusky color of her skin told us all we needed to know. Owen injected epinephrine into Jimena's IV. I kept up with the compressions, hoping the epi would circulate to her heart and give it a jump-start.

After about fifteen long seconds, Owen held out his hand. "Stop, Rees."

I paused. Owen's face had aged ten years since Jimena's arrival. His stethoscope hung off his left shoulder, as listless as Jimena herself.

A beat pulsed on the EKG screen. A second later, another beat pulsed. Even after the epi, her heart rate was still way too slow for an infant.

"We have a pulse," Owen said. "There's a chance."

Nochedrilo sat up in his chair at the wisp of excitement in Owen's voice, his face full of question.

"Restart compressions," Owen directed.

I obeyed. The scene turned surreal. It was a horror show—fluids pumping into Jimena, Owen forcing air down her throat, and me thrusting my hand into her chest repeatedly. No parent should have to witness this gruesome torture, this life-saving modern medicine. But Nochedrilo didn't turn away.

Sister Torres came back to the room without Evelyn.

"Get another dose of epi," Owen ordered.

We repeated the same routine, but Jimena's color slowly purpled. Her lungs just weren't working well enough to get oxygen into her bloodstream.

When we stopped again, her EKG was flatlined. No cardiac activity.

Owen shook his head in disbelief. He stretched his hand, undoubtedly sore from a night of pumping oxygen into Jimena's endotracheal tube. "One more time."

I put a hand on his shoulder and he looked back at me, wanting a wish I couldn't grant. I shook my head and frowned.

Owen looked up at Nochedrilo. "Lo siento."

Nochedrilo wiped away a tear from his eye. The curled his lower lip into his mouth and bit it so hard that it bled. He licked the blood back into his mouth. He stood up abruptly and strode out of the room.

Sister Torres sprang into action, pulling out Jimena's IV. A drop of blackish purple blood exited the wound. "Help me," she ordered. "We have to make her presentable."

Owen pulled out the endotracheal tube and I removed the EKG leads and the pulse oximeter. When we were done, Sister Torres wrapped Jimena in a blanket.

Moments later, Evelyn and Nochedrilo reentered the room. Evelyn's hair was everywhere, sucking into her nose and mouth with every sob. Nochedrilo followed behind in silence, rigid and grim, a firm hand on Evelyn's back.

Evelyn scooped up Jimena, clutching her baby to her chest. She looked at Owen, Sister Torres, and me with wild eyes. Bewildered. Exhausted. Distraught.

Sister Torres said something to them. Evelyn nodded in agreement, but Nochedrilo just stared at Owen.

Evelyn repositioned Jimena's body into a better swaddle. Sister Torres started a prayer with the sign of the cross. Nochedrilo shook his head no and pulled Evelyn toward the door. As they began to leave, Nochedrilo whispered something to his wife. They both turned back to look at the three of us, but didn't say another word.

A minute later, we heard the engine of the old truck rumble to life. Moments later, the sound trailed off into the jungle.

Jimena's parents were understandably heartbroken, but I sensed something more in that parting look they'd given us. "What were they saying?" I asked Sister Torres. "Do they think we caused Jimena's death?"

She nodded, slowly.

Owen gave a low moan. "If the patient survives, thank God. If the patient dies, blame the doctor." He began cleaning his equipment, setting up for the upcoming day's cases.

Sister Torres followed his lead. "I told them we did what we could."

"We did the best anyone could in this situation," Owen clarified.

I told you it was a tragedy. Trying to keep Jimena alive with rudimentary supplies was asking for a miracle. You're in the business of providing medicine, not miracles.

I pushed Lou's useless pep talk off a cliff in the back of my mind. I *wanted* to perform miracles.

"It was a no-win situation," I said.

"It is what it is," Owen replied. Keep moving forward and cope later—an unsaid mantra of the medical world.

"Get some rest," I told him. "We can start the morning cases late. There are some minor procedures I can do with Kat. Straight local."

Owen's only response was a shrug.

I left the room and trudged up the hallway, heavy with exhaustion and gloom.

Maybe Kat will be sitting in the dining area, waiting for you.

It would be great to have someone to share my grief with. Maybe even to share another kiss with. But my spark of hope was smothered by the sight of the dining room, dark and empty.

I walked outside, where the town sat in silence. We were both drained.

Drained and hopeless.

Chapter 12

If racing thoughts are a little hamster running on a wheel, my personal hamster had worn its legs down to bloody stumps. I tried to sleep after I got back to my room, but every few minutes, I glanced over at the clock. My mattress felt like it was made of knots.

I finally gave up, got out of bed and got dressed. I walked outside and back into the building to the kitchen, supposedly to get something to drink. My thirst was just an artifice to run into Kat, though. I'd have settled for anyone, anyone willing to listen and give me a pat on the back. But no luck.

When I went back outside to return to my room, I noticed a truck idling at the corner again, with men climbing into it. In front of that truck sat Nochedrilo's vintage version. He stood behind it, watching the men climb into the back of the other one. As I watched, he whacked one of the men in the back of the head as he passed.

I stepped back against the wall. Nochedrilo hadn't taken the day off to grieve. He hadn't even taken off a few hours. I hurried back to my room, and my mind hurried back to the unbelievable night. The kiss, followed so quickly by tragedy. How could Mother Nature bookend something so exciting with something so tragic? That unexpected kiss from Kat, and then, without a moment to revel in it, the death of an innocent baby? Was this some sort of test?

Images of Jimena's lifeless body and Nochedrilo drawing blood from his own lip flashed through my mind, but it was the thoughts of Kat's kiss that I finally fell asleep to.

***

I showed up late to breakfast, and the room was empty. I didn't have much of an appetite, so I stuck with liquids. Strange to be in a place fertile enough to grow any fruit imaginable and having powdered orange drink as my option. I drank some of the fake juice, put on a fake smile, and headed to the recovery room.

Sister Torres already had patients waiting for us. As soon as Kat saw me, she came over to give me a big hug. Despite our kiss, there was nothing romantic about this hug, which was so long and tight it was clearly an I-heard-what-happened-and-I'm-sorry hug. When she finally let go, she looked up at me. "Are you okay?"

Better than Jimena.

I ignored Lou's snarky, but true, response. "For the most part. We can talk more later," I said.

Kat had moved a small table alongside the recovery room beds and had arranged sterile instrument packs and gloves on it. I had to give her credit; she had an amazing ability to get things ready with almost no training and less oversight. She even had the correct size gloves pulled for me—most impressive.

I grabbed some lidocaine from Owen's supply and filled a syringe for Ziggler and another for myself.

"Looks like we're starting with an EIC," I told her. Keep moving forward.

Kat looked intrigued. "What's an EIC?"

"Epidermal inclusion cyst. It's a blocked oil gland. As the gland produces more oil, it just expands under the skin. They're fun."

"Fun?" Kat asked. "For whom?"

I grinned, my first smile since dinner the night before. "For the surgeon."

Kat smiled back. "There's the real you. Good morning."

"It was a rough night," I said.

"Yeah." Kat paused. "Do you think Nochedrilo will come back with Dr. Yanpa?"

That was a scary thought. Nochedrilo might be interested in a couple thousand dollars' payback of his own.

Or more.

Then I remembered the trucks. "Doubt it. I saw him picking up workers this morning like nothing had happened."

I know you're thinking about how to get that much the money together.

I put aside the thoughts of bribes and revenge as Sister Torres brought in our patients and Ziggler arrived. Soon the lumps-and-bumps clinic was rolling, with both Kat and Sister Torres translating. Kat also kept an eye on both my and Ziggler's cases, but mostly mine.

My patient had a red grape-sized bump on the top of her head protruding upward like one of those lumps on the head of a cartoon character who has just been walloped by a boulder.

Kat looked at it intently. "So how do these glands get blocked?" she asked.

"Bad luck," I said.

Kat tilted her head to the side as if asking for a better answer.

"Don't get me wrong, I'm a big fan of causality," I explained. "It's human nature to want to know why. If we know the cause, we can pretend we have control over it. Joe Schmoe got lung cancer. Of course he did—he smoked like chimney. Jim Bob had a heart attack. Of course he did—he was under constant stress and never exercised."

Kat nodded, which was enough to make me keep going. "But medicine teaches you over and over there are many things beyond control, even when we know exactly why or how they happened. Just look at Jimena. We knew her lungs weren't working, but we couldn't do anything to fix them. All the knowledge in the world can't change that sort of bad luck."

Kat frowned. "But doesn't believing that make things...tolerable? Isn't every death preceded by a moment of futility?"

I shook my head, continuing my examination of our patient's blocked oil gland. "Futility, now there's something a surgeon loathes."

"Inevitability," Kat said.

"Maybe, but no one likes losing." I motioned to our patient's scalp. "No better way to erase the pain of loss than following it up with victory. This EIC will be an easy one."

I switched from philosopher to teacher as I injected along the edges of the outlined ellipse, and then wider around the cyst. "There are only a few real tips to taking out an EIC. First, inject around—not into—the cyst. It's like a little water balloon, only filled with cheesy white debris. Pump anesthetic into it instead of around it, and it swells, creating a very tense water balloon. Then, one wrong move during the dissection, and *pop*, smelly discharge splats you in the face. You only catch a glop of it on your forehead once before learning that lesson for good."

Kat winced. "They smell?"

"Like old shoes." One incision and a few spreads with a mosquito clamp later, I popped out an intact cyst the size of a green grape. The easy ones make a surgeon look good.

An easy victory. I felt a little better. Life would go on.

Kat looked at the cyst with obvious admiration. "Can we cut it open after she's gone?" she whispered.

"Knock your socks off," I told her as I started stitching our patient's wound closed. It wasn't until I missed grabbing the tail of the delicate suture that I realized I wasn't wearing my surgical glasses. I could work without them, but they made it easier to close the edges of skin perfectly.

I finished closing the wound, Sister Torres escorted the patient to the front, and a gloved Kat swooped in to collect the excised EIC.

"While you have fun with that, I'm going to get my loupes," I told her. "I'll be back in a few."

I hadn't even left the procedure room when Kat started laughing. "Ewwww. Stinks like a scummy fish tank," I heard her say to no one in particular.

That woman should have been a doctor.

That woman should be your girlfriend.

Chapter 13

I stepped outside into the late morning sun. A few townsfolk smiled at me as I walked back to my room. There were always people milling about the street, but it never seemed like anything was ever going on. From what I could tell, anyone who didn't take the early morning truck didn't have a nine-to-five job. What did people in Urycu do all day?

Once in my room, I brushed my teeth for the second time that morning. I hated not brushing after eating breakfast, even if I brushed before breakfast. Everyone has idiosyncrasies. What were Kat's?

Maybe she hates toes . . . just the big ones. They look like misplaced thumbs.

I rolled my eyes at Lou's thought. Then, I grabbed my loupes and headed back.

Now the street was completely empty. Maybe the locals had seen me and decided they better all get to work. They didn't want the American catching on to how nice life was in the jungle.

As I approached the front of the building, I spotted Nochedrilo's truck parked kitty-corner from the church. Someone was sitting inside, but I was too far away to see who it was.

I rounded the corner of the building, and a small crowd came into view. About twenty-five feet in front of me stood Owen, Sister Torres at his side. Nochedrilo stood directly in front of Owen, waving his arms and spouting out Spanish so quickly I couldn't catch a word. But the harshness and staccato of his delivery conveyed his unhappiness loud and clear. Three men stood behind Nochedrilo like his own criminal-level Secret Service detail.

I stepped closer. One of the three men behind Nochedrilo locked eyes with me, his hand on the back of his right hip. The international sign for "Don't make me pull this on you." I stopped.

Empty streets. Nochedrilo. Backup bullies.

Revenge.

I could tell Sister Torres was translating Nochedrilo's diatribe for Owen, but I was still too far to hear. As she spoke, she covered her right fist with her left hand. She brought them close to her stomach as if she was trying to hide them. She shifted back and forth as she talked, giving Nochedrilo quick glances as she did.

Owen shook his head in disagreement then looked straight at Nochedrilo. "That's not fair. We did everything we could." He raised a hand, pointed at Nochedrilo, and then immediately lowered his hand again.

I took another step closer. Nochedrilo's backup locked eyes on me again. He was a scruffy sort of guy with bushy hair. When he scowled at me, I froze.

Nochedrilo was yelling at Owen now, red-hot anger flushing his cheeks. He waved both arms up and down, faster and faster. Suddenly, a very large revolver appeared in his right hand, pointed straight at Owen's chest.

"Don't argue," I called to Owen. "Do whatever he wants."

Owen shot me a glance. I recognized his look. It was the same one he'd given me on the way to the OR with Mrs. Childs and her emergency airway. He was going to try his way first.

I had to stop him. I took another step forward, but Nochedrilo's back-up guy pulled out a gun and aimed it at me. That was enough to make me freeze.

Nochedrilo nodded at the two sidekicks on his left. A young man with an uncharacteristically thick mustache grabbed Sister Torres's arm. The other had something in his hands, but it wasn't a gun. The sunlight caught the edge of metal, reminding me of the shiny object I'd seen in someone's hand the first time I'd seen the trucks.

Sister Torres struggled to pull her arm free. "No, no, no, no," she screamed.

Nochedrilo said something to Sister Torres, and she stopped struggling.

"What'd he say?" Owen demanded.

Nochedrilo turned the gun toward Sister Torres and cocked the trigger. She froze.

I didn't know what to do. Even if I knew Spanish, had a weapon, or was standing right next to Owen and Sister Torres, I'd still be helpless.

I looked around for anyone else who could help. The door to the school was opened a crack. I imagined Kat, Shyla, and Ziggler peeking out from behind it.

Stay where you are.

Wasn't anyone here in Urycu on our side?

A tiny, heroic voice in my head said I could somehow get up to the guy next to Nochedrilo, wrestle the gun away from him, and shoot Nochedrilo, all before anyone else could get hurt.

You wouldn't get five feet before getting plugged.

As I debated my next move, Sister Torres reluctantly opened her hand. The man with the shiny object motioned for her to stick her finger into the device, which I could now see looked like a heavy-duty cigar cutter. Now I understood how the Nochedrilo chewed off fingers.

Sister Torres slid her finger into the device, making the sign of the cross with her other hand as she cried, "Te lo ruego" over and over, loud enough that I could hear her clearly. I didn't know the exact meaning of her words, but it was clear she was begging for mercy.

Nochedrilo held his hand up for her to stop.

Owen raised his hands again. "It's not her fault! Stop, please!" His voice broke to a cry. "Your daughter was very sick. There's nothing anyone could have done. Don't punish Sister Torres for trying."

I risked a small step closer. "Take my finger instead, Nochedrilo! Sister Torres was just helping."

Nochedrilo glared at me through slitted eyes. He turned back to Owen, giving him a long look. I watched as Nochedrilo's chest filled with air, then slowly settled as he exhaled.

He's coming to his senses. Deep breath. Relax.

His partners relaxed their stances visibly. Sister Torres, however, did not, as she watched Nochedrilo closely. He said something to her, and her face stiffened.

She looked at Owen reluctantly. "He says you can lose a finger, or fight."

I stepped even closer while Nochedrilo's sidekicks were distracted.

"Alto, alto, alto," I called. At least I knew the Spanish word for stop. "Those aren't the only options."

Owen turned his hands up and to the sides. He shook his head at Sister Torres. "You tell this sick fuck to put the guns down, come inside, and we'll talk this thing out."

"Sick fuck!" Nochedrilo yelled. His posture tightened like a snake about to strike.

"Yeah, sick fuck," Owen raised his own voice in return. "You don't go torturing people just because your daughter died. We were trying to help you."

The day darkened a shade as Nochedrilo whipped the gun back toward Owen.

The pistol roared like a cannon. I covered my ears by instinct, the sound deafening even from a distance.

Owen fell backward to the ground, blood trickling from a hole in the center of his forehead. He exhaled a sick moan as his final breath escaped.

I began to run forward. *Owen.* One of the sidekicks swung toward me, gun aimed at my chest, and I froze yet again.

My heart beat so fiercely in my ringing ears I could barely hear Sister Torres's screams as she broke free of the man holding her and knelt next to Owen. When she reached for his pulse, the man with the finger cutter looked at Nochedrilo.

Nochedrilo waved the tip of the gun towards Sister Torres.

Sister Torres wailed as she bent over Owen's lifeless body. I couldn't help picturing baby Jimena, dead in her mother's arms just hours earlier.

I rushed forward, but before I could get between Sister Torres and Nochedrilo, the man with the cutter grabbed her right wrist and pulled it back toward him. In a flash, the end of her finger fell to the ground. It happened so quickly Sister Torres didn't seem to feel it. Her screams never faltered.

Nochedrilo pointed his gun at Owen again. Even through all the chaos and ringing, I couldn't miss the words he directed toward my friend's body. "Sick fuck," he yelled as Sister Torres pressed her uninjured hand on Owen's carotid.

I wanted to wake up. This couldn't be real. How could this man kill a doctor who was only trying to do good in the world?

Because Owen wouldn't give up a finger.

What?

Better to lose a finger than to lose a head.

I held my hands high to show I was not a threat. "Let me check him," I called as calmly as possible. No more yelling. No more swearing.

The man with the drop on me held his gun steady, his other hand up. Stay there.

I stayed.

Sister Torres bent over Owen, crying and begging. Blood dripped from her partially amputated finger, which she squeezed with her other hand as she sobbed and prayed.

"Let me help them," Ziggler call from the door.

Nochedrilo turned his gun toward Ziggler.

"He'll kill all of you," Sister Torres cried. "Go!"

Ziggler pulled the door closed, and as the sidekicks raced toward it, I took my chance to run.

Zigzag. Zigzag.

I heard another roar of a gun, but this one sounded like bullet hitting wood. The door. Then another shot. The rim of my ear burned, and as I lunged back toward the corner of the school, a bullet hit the wall.

I reached up and felt my ear, but didn't need to see the blood on my hand to know I'd been shot. A voice yelled something in Spanish behind me, but I didn't dare look back.

I rounded the next corner and ran along the backside of my building, wishing I had some sort of weapon in my room. But I couldn't think of anything.

The back door of the church opened. I slowed, expecting one of Nochedrilo's men to cut me off, but Ziggler rushed out with Kat on his heels and Shyla right behind her.

Kat's face flashed relief and then shock and confusion. "Rees!"

I pointed to the end of the road. "There's a path right ahead."

Ziggler let the two women go ahead. I caught up to him, and he turned toward me as we ran. "Is Owen...?"

"Yes." My stomach and heart tried to switch places as I said it.

We plowed into the jungle without a thought as to where we were going, except away. Rain began pelting the leaves. The afternoon showers were ahead of schedule.

As the path narrowed, branches lashed at my arms. The trail sloped steeply downward. At some point we'd hit a road, perhaps the very one we'd driven in on that looped up the hill to Urycu.

After a couple minutes of running, we stopped at a fork in the trail. Ziggler gasped for air. "I wish I were in better shape. Sorry if I'm holding you back."

A sickly Shyla patted his sweaty shoulder. "You're in better shape than I am. This stomach thing has got me wiped out."

Kat pulled gently at her left sleeve with her right hand. The sleeve had been torn on the thorny plants we'd run through. She had little horizontal cuts on her upper arms. It turned out we all did. "What now?" she gasped, as out of breath as Ziggler and Shyla both.

I hesitated. What choices did we have? "This path must hit a road." I said

Ziggler nodded. "Lead the way."

I made my way slowly down the rapidly muddying slope, trying to plant my steps on tree roots, which were few and far between.

Above us, closer up the hill to town, a man shouted down. We'd been found.

"Run, run!" Shyla yelled as she skidded down the trail behind me, pushing for me to go faster.

The ground was too slippery to trust, so I tried to launch myself from tree to tree in the steeper areas. Every few steps, Ziggler grunted the word "Shit."

A gunshot roared from the hill above us.

Kat yelped and fell, and then let out a deep, throaty scream.

She's hit! I turned back, just in time to see Shyla plowing straight toward me. I jumped to the side to let her go by. Ziggler was just behind Shyla, and just behind him was Kat, sliding downhill on her butt, arms flailing.

Farther up the hill, a silhouette skittered and sidestepped downward.

Kat planted a foot against a root, using her momentum to pop herself back onto her feet. But she overshot her balance and fell forward into Ziggler, bringing him down right in front of me. I held my left hand out to him, and he latched onto my wrist as he slid past. I grabbed at a tree with my right hand, my fingernails catching only clumps of bark as Ziggler's momentum yanked me away from the trunk.

Ziggler let go as soon as he realized I couldn't stop him, but it was too late. I splatted into the mud next to Kat, and the three of us began sliding down the slope one after another, like bobsledders riding down a muddy chute, only without the bobsled. My butt bounced off a root. It stung in a way that warned my muscles would be intensely sore in a day or two.

If there is a tomorrow.

I struggled to stay upright, still trying to see if Kat had been shot. I looked for blood, but all I saw was mud.

"Get out of the way!" Ziggler hollered at Shyla ahead of us.

But she couldn't veer in time, and he hit the back of her legs. Shyla fell on top of him with a squeal, the sort of puppy yelp that in any other situation would have been funny. Connected as some kind of muddy clot, the four of us traveled another 30 feet down the watery vein cut into hillside before finally slowing to a stop at a brief flat spot.

Kat held her left shoulder gingerly as she stood, giving it a test shrug. I didn't see any evidence of a bullet wound.

"We've got to keep moving," Ziggler urged as he pulled Shyla up and pushed her toward the trail cutting downward.

Our pursuer stopped at the top of the hill we'd just slid down, steadying himself as if to shoot again.

I pushed Kat forward. "Keep low!" I yelled.

We moved down the hill desperately. The man was close enough that we couldn't just duck into a hiding spot. Our only choice was to outrun him.

The path started to flatten, and through the rain I could see the road ahead.

"When you get there, go right!" Ziggler yelled.

We were only thirty feet from the road when Nochedrilo's truck roared up, stopping just where we'd been heading. We froze and watched as the truck turned and drove away, leaving behind a second man to track us.

I looked back up the hill, where the first man was perched on a ledge looking down at us, gun raised.

"Alto ahí," came a man's voice from behind us. The man from the truck had spotted us. I recognized him now as the one with the goofy black mustache, the one who'd chopped off Sister Torres's finger. But instead of holding his cruel device, he was holding a revolver.

Before we could make a plan, the uphill gunman fired and a bullet cut through the leaves on my right. Ziggler hit the ground as I dove to the side. Kat and Shyla fell flat. The only one left standing was the mustachioed man, and as I watched in a mix of horror and relief, he caught a bullet in the face.

I rolled toward Shyla and Kat, who were already scrambling into the thick vegetation on the side of the trail. Kat's shoe slid off, but she kept going.

As soon as the blasting from uphill stopped, Ziggler crawled down to the dead man near the road and snatched his gun. I wriggled into the trail Kat and Shyla had created as they fled. I looked back at Ziggler.

He stayed on the ground next to the dead man and got into a stable position holding the gun with both hands, arms resting on the chest of the dead man. He raised the gun a fraction of an inch, his face cool and calm, like he'd been in this very situation a thousand times before. He pulled off three quick shots. I admired Ziggler's ability to stay sharp and shoot a gun. I didn't think I could shoot to kill. I couldn't even shoot.

A scream echoed from the hill above us.

"Got him," Ziggler said under his breath. He opened the revolver's chamber and shook his head. "No bullets left." He patted the pockets of the dead man then with a frown shoved the gun into his pants. "Only three bullets? There are four of us."

A moan followed by a raspy yell came from the shooter up the hill. He wasn't dead.

"Let's go," Ziggler called to me quietly as he toward me. I grabbed Kat's lost shoe, and together we followed the trail she and Shyla had made. I didn't know what dangers were still ahead of us, but Kat wasn't going to have to face them half-barefoot it I could help it.

Chapter 14

We only had to follow the trail a hundred feet before finding Kat and Shyla. They stood together, Kat hugging Shyla, both staring at us. The rain had washed most of the mud off them, but they looked bedraggled, like a couple on the news right after a hurricane had destroyed their house. Kat's wet hair was plastered to her head, and a bit of mud still coated her shoeless foot.

I held out her shoe. She looked at the shoe but didn't move. That's when I noticed her normally almond skin was a few shades lighter than normal and her eyes were wide with fear. She let go of Shyla and stepped back to reveal a patch of red blood covering her left breast.

Oh, shit.

A heavy weight hit my heart at Lou's words. I stepped forward quickly. "You're shot! Let me see."

"I'm not," Kat said. She pointed at Shyla, hand pressed to the right side of her neck. Streaks of rain and blood created a gruesome pattern on Shyla's forearm, almost like a barbershop's pole. The black color of her T-shirt mostly obscured the dark, glistening blood soaked into the fabric.

Ziggler hurried forward, too. "What happened?"

"At first I thought a branch snagged me, but I think I was shot in the neck." Shyla spoke calmly and quietly, as if any strain would make the bleeding worse.

Kat pulled her own shirt tight and looked at the stain in disbelief.

"All this blood is yours?" I asked to Shyla.

"Fuck," Ziggler muttered. He nudged me in the back. "It's above the clavicles, your territory."

I snapped into doctor mode and put my left hand on Shyla's. She looked me straight in the eyes. "It's bad," she mouthed, glancing at Kat.

At least Shyla was on her feet and neurologically intact. A bullet to the neck could kill someone instantly. Just seeing her upright was a good prognostic sign.

I gently tugged Shyla's hand out of position and a stream of blood shot out the side of her neck. With every heartbeat, another little spurt of blood arced over her shoulder and onto the nearby foliage.

Kat gave a moan. Looking at her pale face, I would've thought she'd lost more blood than Shyla.

"Kat," I said.

She kept staring at the little spurts.

"Kat!" I snapped.

She looked at me, eyes wide.

"Students who get weak at the sight of blood don't become surgeons. But you're a surgeon at heart. Get over here and hold firm pressure on this."

I stepped to the side to let Kat stand in front of Shyla, and with my left hand, I put Kat's right hand on Shyla's neck. I leaned in toward Kat's ear and whispered, "When I start feeling faint, I bite my tongue, hard."

Color returned to Kat's face, and she stuck her tongue out at me. Blood stained the edge of the tip. She stuck out her elbow to push my hand off of hers. "I got it," she said with a stony confidence I admired.

"What's the verdict?" Ziggler asked.

I didn't want to say what I really thought, but I also didn't want to waste time arguing. "There's no telling how long we're going to be out here. Holding pressure might not be enough."

Shyla looked at me, her lips trembling. I'd never seen her scared, and wished I could make our current reality disappear.

"Fuck. We've got to keep moving, then," Ziggler said.

Kat straightened and pushed her wet hair behind her shoulders. "I can hold her neck."

Compression was a great first step but not a solution. Holding pressure with fingertips wasn't ideal, either. We needed cloth to soak up the leaking blood and, more importantly, to disperse the pressure evenly over Shyla's wound.

But we were covered in mud, lacked supplies, and in no way were prepared for miles of hiking. Kat was wearing a T-shirt and a pair of Shyla's scrub bottoms. Ziggler and I were in light green scrubs. The front half of Shyla's T-shirt was stained with blood, but that wasn't a lot of blood.

My own shirtsleeve was already torn from the thorny branches. I grabbed it with my right hand and yanked, tearing off a strip of fabric. I folded it into a square.

I readied the cloth at the side of Shyla's neck and motioned for Kat to move her hand off the wound. A spurt of blood shot out. I forced myself not to push the fabric down to stop the bleeding again. I needed to evaluate the gash, and letting it bleed a few extra seconds was the only way I could.

Shyla was right. A bullet had torn through the side of her neck, leaving entrance and exit wounds that were almost kissing. It might only be a graze, but it was a deep one. Blood shot from the exit site. Torn pink muscle bulged from the open part of the wound. Standard of care would be an angiogram to see which vessels were damaged. Option two would be a trip to the OR to clean up the wound, tie off the vessel, irrigate it with a boatload of antibiotic solution, and close it up.

Option three: sew it up out here.

I needed my emergency bag.

Ziggler looked back toward the road. "We're all going to get shot if we stay here."

I positioned the square of cloth on the wound. "Hold this," I told Shyla. "Firmly."

Shyla put her hand on top of mine. Her fingers jittered as we swapped positions. I looked her straight in the eyes. "You're going to be fine."

"Promise?" she asked.

I gave her wrist a squeeze. "You know I don't lie."

Shyla nodded almost imperceptibly.

We were too far from Tarapoto to get supplies. Going back into Urycu was my only choice. Traveling back there would be risky. Getting in and out of my room or the church for supplies would be like carrying a raw steak into a lion's den and expecting no one to notice. But I couldn't let Shyla die here like Owen, so I had to try.

The rain started to let up.

I pushed my way through some ferns, still desperately thinking of a way to help Shyla that didn't involve going back to town. "Let's find a place for you two to rest," I told her and Kat. "Maybe a nice tree to hide under while I go back for my suture kit."

Shyla's eyes went wide. "You can't go back. They'll kill you."

"You need stitches. Or I could try an alternative treatment."

"What's the alternative?" Kat asked.

I pointed to a brown wriggling orb underneath a fallen tree. "That."

Kat, Shyla, and Ziggler leaned in for a closer look.

"A ball of ants?" Ziggler asked.

I nodded. "Army ants. The natives used them for sutures. They'd hold an ant so it bit down on both sides of a wound. Once its pinchers dug into the skin, they'd break the ant's body off from the head."

"Not a chance," Shyla said as she started walking.

Finally, that History of Medicine class just paid off.

Together we worked our way up to the trail shooting off our main trail. I'd go back for supplies after I found a safe hiding place for Shyla and Kat. Farther up the hill, the man Ziggler had shot in the neck moaned at us. We ignored him, taking the path that led away from Urycu. We needed some distance from the man. Injured or not, he still had a gun.

We hustled down the path, not knowing how many people were still chasing us or how close they were. After ten minutes, another trail broke off and went downward, probably to the road again.

I stepped off the trail into the brush at the junction, pushing forward until I found a giant tree. Shyla checked the ground for unwelcome critters and then took a seat against the tree. "Here's an alternative. You guys go on ahead, get help, and come back for me," she said.

Kat sat down next to her and leaned her body against Shyla's left shoulder. "I'm not leaving your side."

Shyla looked toward Kat without turning her neck. "I'll be fine if it's meant to be."

Kat's eyes widened. "What do you mean, *if it's meant to be*? There's no meant to be. Those guys mean to kill us and we mean to survive. You just can't throw your arms up in the air and say it's all up to God or destiny or whatever."

Tears cut trails down Kat's muddy cheeks, but she didn't stop to wipe them off. She was too busy shaking her fists in the air. "Fuck fate. We make our own fate, Shy. We're not just going to sit here waiting for whatever's *meant to be*."

Shyla shifted her body toward Kat so she could look at her straight on. "Do you honestly believe that?" she whispered. "That we can take control of our destiny?"

"Of course I do!" Kat burst out in a loud whisper. "This is all shitty circumstance. We can get out of here."

Shyla started to tilt her head to the side, only to wince in pain. "Then why don't *you* take control?"

"I am—" Kat began, then stopped. Shyla waited until a wave of realization crossed Kat's face. I already knew it, but Shyla was a bad ass. Shot in the neck, yet still teaching little sis a lesson about taking control of her own life.

Kat shook her head. "Okay, okay, I get it." She looked up at Ziggler and me and then back to her sister, a tear in her eye yet somehow smiling. "I'd choke you right now if it wouldn't get blood all over my hands."

Shyla smiled back.

Kat crossed her arms. "I'm still staying with you."

Ziggler shook his head. "It's not like the bad guys are going to come with trumpets blaring. Let's go! The longer we stand here, the closer they get."

"What if you guys don't come back?" Kat asked. One look at her face said she was no longer scared but still was planning for the worst.

Ziggler pointed. "If neither of us is back within two hours, take this trail west. Tarapoto's west. I hope by the time you hit a road or town, you'll be well outside the radius of these assholes. When I come back, I'll give a little whistle so you'll know it's me. And keep an ear out for the bad guys. We'll need to know if they end up ahead of us."

Shyla nodded, and I patted her arm. "We'll be back," I promised.

Kat held out a fist and I bumped it straight on with mine. Then she pushed her fist toward Ziggler. He smiled and hit it on top with his own fist.

I gave Shyla a thumbs-up, and she returned it. Part of me wanted to take a moment and tell her how great I thought she was. I felt honored to have worked with her these last few years. But I kept quiet. Saying anything would be admitting I thought one of us wasn't going to make it.

Ziggler and I stepped back up the trail to the fork. "You can't take the trail," he said.

"I won't," I replied. "And you can't come with me. If we both get caught, there's no one left to help them."

He pointed in another direction. "That's why I'll be scouting this trail," he said. He held out his fist sheepishly. "Good luck."

I hit his fist with mine and he smiled faintly. He turned down the other trail and paused. He didn't even turn back to look at me when he said in a quiet voice, "You're all right. Owen made the right choice." He didn't even wait for an answer before going on.

The right choice? Rambo would have been the right choice.

Chapter 15

I moved a few steps up the trail and stopped to cup my hands around my ears. At first listen, the jungle seemed so quiet. No grumble of machinery in the distance, no sounds of humans at work, no trucks chugging along the roads. But after a few moments, the noises of the jungle itself started to come into focus. I could hear leaves dripping water and strange rustles, like the trees shaking themselves dry from the rain. The sounds were random, nothing rhythmic like human footsteps in hot pursuit.

Ziggler tasking Shyla and Kat with a mission to listen was a lot cleverer than just telling them to keep quiet. Listening would keep them quiet, and quiet would keep them safe.

I made a mental map of where I thought we were. We'd run and slid down a hill from the church. Then we turned ninety degrees to the right and gone fairly straight. That made two sides of a triangle. I'd try to travel the hypotenuse, stay off the trails, and end up right near my room. If my angle was too wide, I'd come in at the end of town or miss it altogether. If my angle was too narrow, I'd hit the trail we slid down and risk bumping into someone. The latter somehow seemed safer.

I pushed through a thin patch of branches and started my trail. The rainforest itself was a mixed bag. Some parts were thick and great for hiding; others were thin, leaving me more exposed. At least the thin areas allowed me to see farther and walk faster.

Hey, numbnuts, what about finding your way back?

I looked behind me to see hundreds of trees. If I overshot them on the way back, I could be looking for Shyla and Kat for hours. Undershooting would put me on the same trail as our pursuers. I needed landmarks.

I picked a large tree with a forked trunk as my first marker and headed straight uphill toward it, counting my steps. I froze in fear every time I heard a noise, certain a man with a gun would step out of the brush right in front of me.

When I reached the forked tree, I made a mark in the dirt at the trunk, and for backup, I broke a twig into pieces and lined them in the mark, pointing in the direction I'd just come from. If I had a pen and sticky note, I would have written "66" on it, since that's how many steps away Shyla and Kat sat.

I walked around to the other side of the tree and picked the next landmark—a tree with multiple trunks. There's a saying about not being able to see the forest for the trees. Whoever wrote that one was never lost in a rainforest.

Twenty-nine steps into my next segment, I heard a crackling in the brush about ten feet in front of me. I crouched down and froze. The crackles were quiet and sounded like they were being made by more than one set of feet—maybe two people moving in my direction.

I inhaled slowly; whomever it was seemed close enough that they should have been able to hear my heart pounding against my ribcage. Their distance narrowed to five feet away, but I still couldn't see anyone. I tried to devise a plan of attack, but another part of me wanted to curl up and die. I crouched into a squatting position with my left hand on the ground for balance. Every muscle tensed as if I were a compressed spring, ready to launch.

The brush moved in front of me. My heartbeat pounded so loud inside my head that I wasn't sure I could even hear the movement of the branches.

Thump. Thump.

The leaves a few feet in front of me started to move. I groped the ground, finding a small rock and clutching it in my right fist. I had lousy aim, but it felt comforting to have a weapon. Rocks worked for the Neanderthals.

They're extinct.

A couple feet ahead of me, a furry head poked into view. The animal had a bear cub–shaped head and brown fuzzy fur but a body like a squat dog, and front paws and overall face like a hunting dog's. A second head poked into view.

Great. I survive cocalero gunmen only to be eaten alive by Peruvian Bear Dogs.

I waved my hands at them, trying to tell them to shoo without making a noise.

The first one yawned. A sharp set of white canines glimmered in the scattered light poking through the gaps in the canopy. The second one looked at me curiously and crept forward.

All my hiking training regarding animal encounters came down to one piece of advice: make yourself big and make lots of noise. Sitting crouched in fear and silence was not an option, even when hiding from men hunting you.

I stood up partway and spread my arms wide. I bared my teeth. The creature closest to me tilted its head sideways. I once had a dog that did the same thing when I'd give it commands it didn't understand. These creatures had to be some sort of species of wild dog.

I stood even taller, waving my arms toward them, trying not to bump any branches. I even growled a little.

A distinct crack of a tree branch snapping interrupted the standoff. The closer one looked back at his partner and crept off toward the sound of the noise. The other one gave me a final inquisitive look before following his friend back into the greenery.

I vowed to do more research before ever going anywhere again.

I collapsed back onto the ground, sitting and waiting for any more sounds. This was all too much. Owen. Dead!

My soft palate tightened up and a knot twisted itself somewhere behind my tongue. Tears fell from my eyes onto the ground. I wanted to sob, I wanted to scream in anger and disbelief, I wanted to bawl, but instead I slumped in silence, stifling my crying with shudders.

After a blubbery minute, Lou spoke up. *Get up. This isn't over.*

I wished I could have done something truly heroic to save Owen, something that would have prevented the tragedy.

There was nothing you could do. I wouldn't have let you try anything stupid.

What? You don't control me. I control you.

Are you sure? Who do you think keeps you calm when the shit hits the fan? You know what I'm talking about—that wave of serenity that comes over you and steadies your hand even when everyone else in the room is loading their shorts and the patient is trying to die? That's me.

I knew that feeling. Calm. Rational.

I pushed myself up out of the mud.

There's one more thing you're forgetting.

What?

Hypothermia.

Forgotten? Yes. Can people suffer hypothermia in the Amazon jungle?

Why not?

I reasoned it out. The temperature dropped into the sixties overnight, and our clothes were wet from the rain. We didn't have blankets, food, or any other way to heat ourselves. A wet human body loses heat twenty-five times faster than a dry one. I wasn't just grabbing supplies to help Shyla; I had to get supplies to save all of us.

I hiked to the edge of Urycu without any more wildlife interludes save a never-ending trail of leaf-cutter ants. I came out into town just down from where I wanted to be. The barren streets seemed to be a warning sign, so I stayed in the jungle as I worked my way along the periphery of the town to the trailhead by my room. When I got there, I walked carefully to the front of the church along the side abutting the jungle. I wanted to see who was there. I wanted to see if Owen was still lying there, or Sister Torres.

The truck the men had climbed into in the wee hours was in front of the church. Owen's body was gone. The door to the church was propped open, but no one was in sight. A few boxes were lined up next to the church. I recognized one of them from the recovery room. The bad guys were stealing our supplies.

Dr. Yanpa walked out carrying a box, which he dropped with the others before going back into the church. Then Sister Torres came out dragging along a box, her injured hand wrapped in gauze. When she stood, she wiped a tear from the corner of her eye with the back of her wrist.

"Pssst," I hissed.

She spun toward me and flashed me an open hand. *Wait.* She

stepped back, looked into the church, and then turned slowly to look down the street. The coast was clear.

She skirted over to the edge of the jungle. "You have to get out of here, Dr. Rees. Nochedrilo wants to kill all of you. He told me when your truck comes next week, I must tell Mila you went into the jungle on a hike and never came back."

Which would work if we were all dead. Tourists lost and never found in the Amazon.

"I need some suture supplies," I said. "Shyla's been shot."

Sister Torres glanced back over her shoulder. "I can't. Dr. Yanpa is in back choosing what he wants. Maybe if you wait here until he leaves?"

What dedication to patient care!

"It's not safe to wait," I said. "I have to get back to the others. I'll check my room."

"Nochedrilo is Urycu's problem, not yours," Sister Torres said softly. "I had hoped you could avoid getting pulled into our trouble." She wrapped her right hand over the bandages on her left in the form of prayer. "Be quiet, and God be with you."

"Thank you for trying to protect us," I said. I squeezed her shoulders with my hands rather than risk giving her a full hug and then I retreated back into the jungle.

Bastard is stealing your equipment.

First things first: Save Shyla and escape to Tarapoto.

Then come back with cavalry and bust this butthole so-called doctor along with Nochedrilo.

I moved a little further into the trees and toward the back of the church. The dirt road to my room was empty but the door was open. The doc had probably already looted it.

I hope your emergency pack is still there.

What about the townspeople? Would they holler if they saw me? Were only a few people hunting us, or the whole town? The locals seemed nice enough, but now that there was trouble, maybe killing all of us might be the easiest option. No faster way to get Nochedrilo to calm down.

The longer you debate and worry, the more blood oozes from Shyla's neck. And the longer you take, the higher the chance they get found. These guys are wolves. They can smell the blood. So get a move on.

I tried to move quickly and casually toward my room, not that anyone would mistake a giant white guy for a local. I stepped silently through the open door, not touching it for fear of making it creak.

A man sat on the floor next to my backpack, back to me and so enthralled with whatever he was holding that he didn't notice me. His rifle was leaning against the wall about a foot away from the door. I picked it up slowly and silently. I didn't know anything about rifles, but I'd seen enough Westerns to check the safety and pull back on the hammer.

I didn't want to shoot him. The sound of a gunshot would bring the other men running. But I needed the medicine bag, and one holler from this guy would also alert the others. I needed a way to keep him quiet *and* alive.

I pushed the safety off.

It clicked.

The man recognized the sound and turned his head slowly toward me.

As his body twisted, I saw my Rubik's Cube in his hand. Part of me wanted to laugh, and another part wanted to cry. This guy's buddies were prowling the jungle looking to kill us while he was trying to solve a children's puzzle, happy as could be.

"Silencio." I didn't know if it was Spanish or a Harry Potter spell.

The man put his arms up, Rubik's Cube still in hand. He knew the routine.

I wanted him to lie down but had no idea how to say it in Spanish. I motioned to the floor with the barrel of the gun instead.

He dropped the Rubik's Cube and then put himself flat on the floor with his hands behind his neck.

I spotted my emergency medicine bag next to the backpack. I almost snatched it and ran, but I still had one problem: how to flee without this man screaming for help. I couldn't shoot him, and it had nothing to do with making noise. I was incapable of killing a man, even a bad one. But I could knock him out with one good hit of the gun's stock.

I turned the gun around, grabbing the barrel tightly and pulling it back. I couldn't help wincing in anticipation of the man's pain.

Put the safety on.

I paused.

Owen's pouch of extra morphine lay on the floor next to my own emergency kit. The idea that we needed to protect it from Kat-the-possible-drug-addict seemed laughable now. But thanks to Owen, I now had an alternative to bludgeoning this guy.

I put one foot on his back and tucked the gun under my left arm. I pulled the bag toward me, unzipping it so I could grab the syringes and bottles inside. Once I drew up the morphine, I knelt on my captive's back. With my left hand, I held the gun propped on the back of his neck.

The way the man's head was turned made his external jugular vein bulge. The EJ is the vein that pops out on the side of an angry man's neck, or in this case, on the neck of a slender man lying on the ground.

He spied the needle and let out a quiet cry.

"Shhh!" I pushed the gun into the back of his neck. "Dorme. No muerto." I knew I had at least one of those words correct, solely because I liked the Day of the Dead—at least the part about a bunch of cool little skeletons dressed up like normal people.

The man closed his eyes and pretended he was already asleep. He must have believed me; if I were in his place, I would've been screaming like a madman.

I stuck the needle through his skin, pulling back a little on the plunger with my thumb. As soon as a drop of blood entered the clear liquid in the syringe, I pushed the plunger down. The morphine entered his vein easily. I withdrew the needle and threw the syringe aside.

Then I waited. It felt like an eternity before the man's breathing slowed. Enough time for me to wonder what the hell I was doing there. How had all of this happened? There was no use dwelling on it now, so I moved onto something more relevant and made a mental list of the supplies I needed to grab.

When the man finally fell asleep, I got to work collecting what I could. I packed the few granola bars I had into the medicine bag and switched my regular shoes for hiking shoes. I pulled most of my T-shirts and underwear out of the backpack to make room for more important things, like the blanket off the bed. I scurried into the bathroom and ripped the shower curtain off the rod. Next I grabbed my clear plastic toiletry bag and dumped everything except the toothpaste and insect repellant. I put the candle and matches from the desk inside the plastic bag, too, then sealed it, folded the shower curtain around it and shoved the wad into the pack.

I removed my wet scrub top and put on a dry T-shirt and a brown raincoat. Then I swapped my bottoms for a pair of quick-dry hiking pants. I put all my other weatherproof clothes into the bag for the others.

I found my cell phone. Hopefully we'd find service long before Tarapoto.

Next time we go anywhere, we splurge on one of those satellite phones.

"You bet," I mumbled as I put the phone into my emergency medicine bag and shoved it into the backpack.

The unconscious man sighed. When it took a few seconds for him to take another breath, I began counting. About eight breaths a minute. A little slow. A bigger dose, and I could have knocked out his drive to breathe altogether.

I grabbed the one unopened bottle of water I had and shoved it into the side pocket of the pack. I picked up the half-empty bottle at the side of my bed and guzzled the remaining water inside before refilling it from the sink and sticking it on the other side.

Time to go. I strapped on the backpack and picked up the gun in one hand. Then I reached down and scooped up the Rubik's Cube with my other, for no real reason besides not wanting to leave my unconscious assailant a keepsake.

Yeah, don't let that bastard tease his mind on your dime.

As I was about the exit the room, a soccer ball rolled past the door. A kid stepped into view. When he saw me, he froze.

I froze, too.

The boy looked up at me, at the gun, and then back at me.

One peep from this kid and the men would come running. I glanced over the top of the boy at the jungle's edge and debated sprinting to it. One good shove would knock the kid flat on his back and I'd be past him and into the undergrowth before he could yell.

I lowered my gaze to the boy. He had a row of sutures across his forehead. Sin Suerte.

Sin looked at me, paralyzed, mentally debating what to do. His eyes lowered from my face to the gun and then drifted to my left hand.

The Rubik's Cube. I held it out for him and smiled.

The boy's paralysis broke. He took the toy from me, his face blooming into a wide grin. His smile said he was now the proud owner of the coolest toy in town.

I held up my fingers to my lips, saying, "shhh." Did they use that gesture in Peru?

Sin Suerte pointed one hopping arm to the rainforest. "Escondete! Escondete!" He wanted me to get back under the cover of the jungle, which was exactly what I wanted, too.

I ran to the edge of the tree line. When I turned back to make sure no one had seen him help me, he gave me a little wave. I gave him the thumbs-up.

He turned his wave into a thumbs-up of his own. Face beaming, he held the Rubik's Cube up with one arm like it was an Olympic gold medal. He took a few triumphant steps and then ran off after his soccer ball.

I stepped off the trail and began looking for my first landmark: the three-trunked tree.

Chapter 16

On the steeper parts of the downhill, I found footprints where my shoes had dug into the mud on the way up. I welcomed the reassurance that I was on the right trail, but at the same time, it scared me how easily we could be tracked. If my solo footprints were so heavy and obvious, the four of us together were leaving a trail like a herd of elephants as we trampled our way through the rainforest.

When I'd first stepped into the jungle from the town, I felt safe under its cover. But as I got closer to the others, I felt fear. Any sound could be our pursuers closing in. The gun provided little security, because if I had to use it, that meant someone was actively trying to kill me.

I stopped more often to listen, but didn't hear anything that sounded like men hell-bent on killing us. The buzz of insects filled the air intermittently, and a couple of them even sought a meal on my arms before meeting the Slapping Hand of Death. I pushed forward slowly through the thick branches and muggy air. Sweat saturated the back of my shirt where the backpack pressed against me. I begged for a breeze, but this was not a day for wishes to come true.

When I got to the edge of the trail, I stopped and listened for a good minute before stepping out onto it. There was a low chance no one was actually out here. But there was also a high chance Nochedrilo had put together a hunting party and was on his way. He already proved himself to be ruthless, and a man like that could be as unrelenting and maddening as athlete's foot when pursuing his prey.

When I finally stepped out onto the trail, I didn't recognize where I was. I walked a minute in the direction away from the church before beginning to worry that I'd gone too far, or was headed the wrong way. I wanted to shout out to Kat and Shyla but didn't dare.

A minute later, I found the offshoot on the left side of the trail, the one Ziggler had gone to explore. If Kat and Shyla had been able to stay hidden, they weren't far away.

As I approached, I whispered sharply, "Kat? Shyla?" I didn't want them to assume I was one of the bad guys and have them bludgeon me with sticks as I pushed through the brush toward them, but I also wasn't a whistler like Ziggler.

"Here," Kat answered quietly from behind their tree. They'd slid around to the backside to keep out of sight.

Shyla was leaning against the tree, eyes closed. Dark circles rimmed her lower eyelids like a football player's eye black, but hers were au naturel. Her right hand was pressed against the side of her neck and she'd bent her leg so her knee propped up her elbow. Blood stained her makeshift bandage, but it wasn't dripping. *Yes.*

My subconscious relaxed as a body-wide muscle tension lifted. Shyla wasn't dying. Kat was filthy, but she looked happy to see me. Even more, she looked energized, ready for anything, which boosted my confidence.

I unstrapped the backpack. "Where's Ziggler?"

"He either ditched us, got caught, or is taking his sweet time," Kat said as she ran her fingers through her thick, muddy hair. The rain hadn't lasted long enough to wash away all evidence of our human mudslide.

We could clean up later. Right now, I needed to sew up Shyla's wound. Years ago, an older surgical resident had told me, "Start every case by setting yourself up for success." For that particular ear case through a microscope, that meant taking a few minutes to adjust the chair, the microscope, and the patient's position to minimize distractions during surgery. As I crouched at Shyla's right side now, I knew I wasn't flexible enough to hold the squatting position as I sewed her wound. I didn't have a table, a chair, or a bed, though, and I didn't want Shyla to lie down in the mud. I looked around for alternatives.

"There's a fallen tree just down this hill," Kat said.

I like mind readers.

The broken trunk sloped downward from its stump. Kat was right. We had an OR table. I took off my rain jacket and spread it across the tree trunk. I motioned to Shyla to sit on it. Then, I positioned Kat in front of her sister so I could work on Shyla's neck from behind her right shoulder. With the neighboring trunk serving as a table, I set up my instruments on their sterile wrappers and drew some local anesthetic up in a syringe.

I frowned at Shyla. "Sorry, this is going to hurt."

She waved me off. "Do whatever you have to do. You're the doc."

Your favorite line.

Shyla knew I loved it when patients gave me permission to do my job. This was a different world, but I tried to ignore the circumstances, acting like I had all the time in the world and we weren't being hunted by brutal murderers. *Proceed slowly whenever possible*, I reminded myself as I injected gently and widely around the area where Shyla was holding pressure. She didn't flinch.

Neither did Kat.

"How can I help?" she asked.

I wiped Shyla's skin with a couple alcohol pads. "Hold the scissors and cut the sutures for me. Don't let the tips touch anything else. I want to maintain sterility as much as possible." I opened a set of sterile gloves, put on the right one, and used it to hand Kat the scissors.

Kat held the scissors in one hand and Shyla's hand in her other. Her focused gaze suggested she'd distanced herself from the fact that the wound was her sister's, a necessary step to clear the mind of fear and misjudgment. It wasn't indifference; it was the way a true surgeon sees a wound—fascinating and sacred in itself.

I instructed Shyla to pull her hand from the wound. The moment she moved her hand, I gave the skin under the strip of cloth a quick wipe with the alcohol as blood squirted from the wound. I put on my left glove then spread my left thumb and index finger on the skin below and above the wound to open it. With my right hand, I probed the wound with a forceps.

I didn't dare look at Shyla's face to see if the local was working. It didn't matter. A stream of blood jetted from a small artery, landing on my arm. I grabbed the nicked artery with the forceps and shifted them to my left hand. No more bleeding.

I loaded up my only dissolvable suture; it would be the one to go around the damaged vessel. The other sutures were nylon, good for closing the skin.

I put the needle through the tissue under the exposed artery and then looped it around again a little farther away. The suture created a figure eight around the vessel. I let go of the vessel with my left hand and tucked the forceps into my palm. One last blast of blood spurted out before I cinched the suture around the vessel and tied it off.

"He got it," Kat told Shyla.

I finished tying the knot and held the suture up. "Little tail."

Kat put the tip of the scissors on the suture, slid down to the knot, angled upward a millimeter, and cut. Short tails. She must've seen Ziggler and I do that during the thyroid case.

I switched to the nylon suture to close Shyla's skin. Nylon was a great choice for a less-than-sterile wound closure. Braided sutures have tiny spaces bacteria can nestle into, out of reach of the immune system. Nylon is a solid cord with nowhere for bugs to hide.

I finished the layer of black nylon suture, giving Shyla's neck a slight Frankenstein's monster look. I lathered on some antibiotic ointment, and then covered the wound with an adhesive bandage.

Leaves and branches rustled behind me. "It's about time you showed up," I said, glad the four of us were safely back together.

Kat shook her head frantically and I knew. It wasn't Ziggler.

"Don't move," a Peruvian-accented male voice said. "Put your hands up."

I raised my hands, still gloved, high. Shyla and Kat did the same. I turned to see a skinny man I didn't recognize, wearing a brown vest and holding a pistol. Lou was right. The wolves were hungry and could smell the blood. We were done for.

"Turn around," the wolf ordered.

Shyla and I slowly turned. The man hardly had any mud on him. Nochedrilo must have recruited him for the hunt after discovering his first two henchmen had been shot.

He waved his gun at Shyla. "Off the tree."

When she slid down from her perch, he pointed the tip of the gun back up the hill. "This way."

I reached down to grab my backpack. The rifle was farther away,

131

leaning against the tree stump. I glanced at it, but didn't dare attempt to dive for it.

"Leave the bag," the man ordered.

I looked at my pack. I should've been hiking in the Sierras with that pack on my back. What I wouldn't give to teleport myself and the team to some middle-of-nowhere California wilderness. But I couldn't, so I slumped my way past our captor and back up the hill. He grabbed the rifle, leaving my backpack behind.

We followed our footsteps back toward Urycu, the gunman following a few steps behind.

"What can we do?" Kat muttered from in front of me.

"Walk slowly," I answered. That would at least give us time to think.

A minute later, Kat stumbled on an exposed root, letting out a high-pitched yelp and falling to the ground. She rubbed at her ankle, but our captor waved his gun again and told her to get up. She started back up the hill, her pace glacial.

When I'm operating hours can pass like minutes. This was just the opposite. Every minute felt like an hour. I scanned through scenarios, first of what would happen to us when we get back to town. I couldn't bare the idea of Kat and Shyla being shot. I needed a plan. Maybe going up the hill near the church was the best time to fight back. The ground was slippery, he'd be watching his feet more than watching us while navigating up the slope. That would be the time to lunge after him.

Barely a couple minutes later, the bushes behind us rustled. It sounded like a horse breaking through the brush. I whipped around to see Ziggler burst out like a lineman going for the quarterback sack. His right arm smashed down on the gunman's arm like he was trying to strip the ball. Next Ziggler wrapped his left arm around the man's torso and plowed his upper chest into the man's left shoulder. Chin tucked, Ziggler planted his head into the nape of the man's neck.

The rifle went flying. The man spun to his right as Ziggler drove him into the ground in one of those tackles that got replayed on the evening news sports highlights. A bone-rattling, concussion-causing takedown. As the two of them tumbled into the brush, a gunshot exploded, followed by the sound of snapping branches and a loud grunt.

I snatched the rifle off the ground and ran into the opening the men had plowed into the bushes. Ziggler was lying flat on top of the other man, who was facedown. Neither was moving. Had we just lost Ziggler, too?

A pistol was stuck in the mud a few inches from the gunman's hand. I slid down the hill and threw myself on his right arm before yanking the gun from the mud and tossing it aside.

Kat grabbed the gun before it landed.

"Don't shoot," I barked as Shyla came up behind Kat, holding the rifle.

Ziggler pushed himself up and groaned. The man underneath him didn't move at all. I moved my hand to his wrist and felt for a pulse. I thought I felt a distant beat, but maybe not. At least Ziggler was alive.

Ziggler rolled the guy over. The front part of his skull was sunken in, and a tree branch a quarter-inch thick protruded from his right eye. The other end of the branch had broken off. The left eye was already a dead stare.

Shyla gasped.

"Holy fuck," Kat blurted. Then she barfed, thin vomit spraying the plants around her. Her face turned red and she quickly wiped her lips off with the back of the hand not holding the pistol.

"He's dead," I said.

Ziggler winced. "And I'm shot." He leaned back and held up his right leg, shin punctured with a bloody hole. I leaped over to examine it. No exit wound, and not much oozing.

Shyla stepped up next to me in nurse-mode, her own injury already forgotten. "You okay?"

"It hurts like a motherfucker and we're being hunted to death, but other than that, things are pretty great," Ziggler said.

"I've got morphine and bandages in my backpack," I offered.

Ziggler looked around. "Where is your backpack?"

Right. "Back where he found us," I answered.

Kat held the pistol up in the air. "What do I do with this?"

Ziggler took it from her and looked in the barrel. "This thing's full of mud, and it's an old gun, anyway. Too risky. It might blow up in your face." He threw it into the brush.

Before we headed back downhill, Ziggler gave the dead guy a quick pat-down. Other than a bit of money in his pocket and a handful of bullets, he had nothing of use. Ziggler took one last look at the body and grunted, "Let's go."

After twenty minutes of careful backtracking, we found our impromptu surgical area and my pack. As Kat checked Shyla's bandage and I collected my supplies to repack into the bag, Ziggler looked over at me. "Save the morphine. I need to be lucid for whatever happens next, so just bandage me up and let's get the hell out of here."

I wanted to argue. It's better to take medicine before pain grabs hold than to try to catch up. But Ziggler seemed like one of those guys who didn't feel pain—at least not physical pain.

I wiped the area near his wound with a little alcohol. Then I used my last antibiotic packet to cover the hole with ointment before wrapping it with a roll of gauze. No telling what was going on in there. The bullet could be wedged in bone, creating a semi-unstable fracture. It could have ricocheted off the bone and be sitting in muscle on either side of the bone. Ziggler was right to want to get moving now before the muscle got really inflamed, or worse, infected. I had antibiotic pills, but only one course, and there was a chance Shyla might need it, too. The faster we could get to Tarapoto, the better for both of them.

When we got back to the westward trail, we sat quietly for a minute to listen for any other potential followers. But if the gunshot hadn't gotten them all running, maybe there weren't that many of them still tracking us.

"What if we took the trail Rees used to go back up to Urycu," Shyla proposed. "We could hide by the edge of town for a couple days until Mila and the trucks come back for us."

Ziggler shook his head. "We don't know who we can trust there, and we don't want to put Sister Torres in any more danger. And as soon as we get desperate for food, we'd have to steal from the townspeople. We can't do that."

Kat nodded in agreement.

I liked the idea of being safe in the village, but it wasn't ideal. Was there a vehicle in the town we could take? I thought of the truck that had picked up the workers in the early morning. Could we steal it from under Nochedrilo's nose and race to Tarapoto without getting caught?

I sighed. "Ziggler's right. We can't stay here. We'd get to Tarapoto faster if we walked. I'll bet we can get there in two days if this trail goes as the crow flies."

Kat linked her arm with Shyla's. "Into the unknown, then."

I leaned in close to Ziggler as we started on the trail in the direction on Tarapoto. "Did you learn anything on your expedition?"

Ziggler limped alongside me. "Yeah. I learned that when I get back home, I'm going to get ahold of my lawyer, and even if it costs every dollar I have, I'm going to find a way to get more time with my kids. My wife and her lawyer are nothing compared to this Nochedrilo bastard."

***

We'd been walking for half an hour, taking turns using the rifle to clear the thin brush across the trail with heavy swings, when Shyla stopped unexpectedly. "Look," she whispered.

We all froze. I didn't hear anything, but I was in the front of the line. I'd been so focused on pushing a way forward through the overgrown trail that I hadn't spent much time looking to the sides or pausing to listen for anyone sneaking up from behind.

Shyla pointed at a tree to the left of the trail. "There's a toucan."

I let out a quiet laugh and my heart slowed to a normal pace.

A colorful bird with a red stripe across his yellow and black chest and a big green beak with an orange tip perched on a branch above us. His eye had a green spot around it surrounded by yellow feathers. He sat there like it was no big deal to be one of the most coveted sights for exploring tourists.

You should hear the toucan's thoughts: Did you see those humans chasing each other with guns? A bunch of freaks all rushing to meet the Reaper. Life is hard enough. Why don't they relax in a tree? Soak up some sun. Eat a few bugs.

"This might be the only moment of the trip I tell my kids about," Ziggler said. "But we need to keep moving."

I took one last glance at the toucan and then swung the backpack off. "We should have a snack first. I've got a few granola bars and two bottles of water."

Kat stared up at the toucan. "We should save what we have till dark and see what we can find in the jungle as we walk."

I looked around. We were surrounded by lush vegetation, but unless I saw a head of romaine poking out of the ground, I doubted I could confidently identify any safe food.

Ziggler nodded slowly. "You're right."

Kat smiled. "What did you say?"

"I got shot in the leg. Doesn't that grant me a reprieve from being an asshole?" Ziggler asked.

Kat smiled wider.

Shyla pointed at an exceptionally large leaf. "I saw a movie once where they used big leaves like a funnel to drink rainwater out of." She tugged on a nearby leaf, still wet with rain, and rolled the edges up. "They just tapped the leaf, and the water poured out the end right into their mouths."

She positioned her mouth under the funnel she'd just created. Then she gave the leaf's branch a good rustle. As a few drops of water trickled down the leaf, something black rolled straight into Shyla's mouth. She jumped back at the shock of something solid hitting her tongue, spitting the object onto the ground. A black beetle twitched upside down for a few strokes and then righted itself. Shyla grimaced and spat as it crawled away to safety. "Why are there so many bugs here?"

Kat and I started laughing, and even Ziggler chuckled.

Shyla gave her sister a long look. "It isn't funny."

Kat wrinkled her mouth. "It's funny."

"It is pretty funny," Ziggler agreed.

Kat gave me a glance. A secret acknowledgment. Ziggler was finally warming up to her.

I pulled the unopened bottle of water out of my pack and handed it to Shyla. "Try this. I've got a second bottle, but it's filled with tap water from Urycu, so it may not be safe."

Shyla took a long swig from the bottle. "Still better than beetle water."

Kat took the bottle from Shyla and looked at it appraisingly. "We can use water from the leaves to refill this when it's empty, too."

We unanimously agreed we'd go as long as we could without drinking any ground water. The Amazon was known for parasites.

Nochedrilo didn't even need to chase us. The odds were high we wouldn't make it out of the jungle alive, and even if we did, we'd be infested or injured by something out here.

Regardless of the dangers ahead, we had no choice but to keep going.

Chapter 17

I stayed at the front of the group for as long as I could. Ziggler was slowing; his leg had to hurt, but he refused pain meds. And Shyla couldn't lead; I didn't want her doing anything as strenuous as whacking foliage with a rifle.

I spied a large, hairy spider crawling under a large leaf.

He's probably one of those wandering spiders Sister Torres warned about. Look at him. He doesn't look like he knows where the fuck he's going, either.

I started stomping the ground with every step, to clear brush and also scare away any snakes or spiders. Some areas were thick with thorny plants, too, and I did what I could to clear them or go around, but the sides of my arms were taking a lashing. It always seemed like we were on a trail, but one that was increasingly overgrown the farther we got from Urycu.

A couple hours later, I stopped and held up a hand. "Hear that?"

The others stopped, too.

A sound like static emanated from ahead of us. It reminded me of the white-noise generator I'd once tried as a sleep aid. Turned out I liked a fan better. The noise generator was too loud, and it sounded too much like running water. Every time I woke up I had to run to the bathroom.

"Sounds like a river," Kat said.

"Maybe there'll be people on a boat." Shyla's voice rose with hope. She pushed forward a bit faster than before.

The path ended at a muddy ledge, a wide river running about eight feet below us. Upstream a small waterfall, maybe thirty feet high, was the source of the noise. Under other circumstances, we would have been snapping photos of the water cascading over mossy rocks, breaking and dividing into separate little paths. The branching waters reminded me of my life. I thought I was going one way only to end up going another, I sure didn't think I'd end up here.

If you follow them, they come back together. Just keep moving forward.

"Cool," Kat said, with an awe I just couldn't share.

"Look here." Ziggler pointed to a short tree just downstream, bushy, and maybe only ten feet tall. It was covered by another viny plant bearing purplish-red fruits. Their shiny, smooth skin made them look like hard cherries, or small pomegranates.

"What's that?" I asked.

"Passion fruit." Ziggler already had a large one in his hand. He gave it a quick wipe on his shirt, which was probably dirtier than the fruit itself, but it was the thought that counted. He tore at it with his hands in a ripping motion until the fruit broke open. He sucked out the seedy yellow insides with a triumphant slurp.

He puckered his lips a little and winced. "Tart." He went back for another bite. "Not bad."

Shyla, Kat, and I joined him. I'd never had passion fruit before. The center didn't look appetizing, but I liked the zing it had, like those sour gummy bears.

"I guess this is dinner," Shyla said.

"I've had worse," Ziggler replied.

Kat looked out at the river. "Too bad we can't catch some fish."

Dangle Ziggler's bloody pant leg in there.

How about being serious for once?

The water flowed by at a decent speed. The waterfall would be the best place to fill the water bottles if necessary. Moving water supposedly had fewer parasites.

In all likelihood, the passion fruit was probably our main source of hydration for the evening unless another rainstorm came along. I opened the backpack and started packing fruit into it. "These might be breakfast, too."

Ziggler patted his stomach. "That's good. I've been trying to cut back on bacon."

Shyla and Kat gave a good laugh. Things were somehow all right, even with Owen dead and Nochedrilo after us. Ziggler somehow seemed happier, despite being injured and in pain. Kat wasn't crazy. No one was panicking. We were a team, a team of survivors.

The mud tried to suck my shoes off as I walked around the tree. A large cluster of fruits hung just past the limits of my reach on the side of the tree facing the river. I held the backpack out to my left as a counterbalance as I leaned right.

"Here, hold my hand," Kat offered.

I slipped my left hand through the top loop of the backpack and then grabbed her hand. The extra weight gave me confidence to reach out and grab the fruit. I pulled one down, dropping it into the front of the bag before reaching for another.

As I shifted back to the right, my foot sank a couple inches into the mud. A split second later the ground below me fell away.

Kat tried to hold on, but the ground liquefied under her as well. The two of us slid down the muddy embankment. I clawed futilely at the muddy wall with my right hand but kept my left hand clamped on the backpack.

I splashed into the river and Kat plunged in next to me. I didn't dare let go of the bag, but my wet clothes and shoes made it a struggle to stay afloat.

I tried to swim against the current. I inhaled a gulp of water and tried to hack it out. Parasites.

There wasn't a shore on our side of the river, just a drop-off. Upstream, Kat was treading water, watching me. In the distance, Shyla and Ziggler stared in disbelief. I rolled onto my back and started kicking.

Kat swam to my side. "Do we have to worry about piranhas?"

"It doesn't make a difference if we worry or not. We're already in." Parasites trying to swim into my orifices scared me a lot more than piranhas.

"That's not reassuring," Kat said.

The sound of rushing water grew louder as we drifted downstream.

"Is that another . . . ?" Kat started.

"Waterfall!" I hollered. A few hundred feet downstream, the river disappeared. The line of trees along the river stopped at the same point. It was like the end of a flat world. I'd been so focused on the waterfall upstream, I hadn't noticed the downstream one.

"Get to the other side!" I yelled.

On the opposite shore, the jungle sloped into the river without any ledges. Kat started doing the freestyle toward the shore. But the current was still taking her downstream. I yelled to get her attention, but she couldn't hear me as she swam.

I tried to swim to her but couldn't make quick progress with the backpack in my hand. Still, I couldn't let it go. It held our phone, matches, and food. I rolled onto my back and started kicking upstream. At the same time, I reached into the bag and pulled out a passion fruit. I took aim for Kat's head.

A little to the right.

I threw it. The fruit plunged into the water just left of her.

I told you so.

I reloaded and tried again, and this time, the fruit pegged her in the head.

Kat stopped swimming, turned to where she expected me to be and then turned farther until she found me. "Something's in here."

"That was me. Can you swim with me? This bag is weighing me down."

Kat swam over. "Put it on backwards. Then you can do the freestyle too."

Good idea. I closed the bag and put it on.

The two of us inched our way to the far shore. The river started to narrow, which helped make the shore closer, but water flows faster in a narrow river.

Between strokes, I heard Shyla and Ziggler yelling for us to swim harder.

My hands finally hit the bottom of the river as I approached shore. I put a foot down and my foot sank into the mud and took hold. I reached back for Kat, pushing her onto the riverbank before crawling out myself.

I retched out the last bit of the water I'd inhaled in the river.

"You okay?" Kat asked.

"No."

"What's wrong?"

I flopped onto the muddy bank. "Nothing. It's just...everything."

Kat scooted to my side and put a hand on my back, giving it a light massage. "Yeah, but you're doing great. It won't be long before you're back in your clinic."

It sounded like something Shyla would say to comfort me. I sat up.

Shyla and Ziggler were on the other side of the river, stuffing their pockets full of fruit before moving upstream to try to cross where the river was wider and slower. Shyla used a long stick to test the depth in front of her.

Ziggler held the rifle in his right hand and locked his left arm with Shyla's right. Watching them was like watching an accident waiting to happen.

Kat nestled next to me like we were kids sitting on the curb watching a parade go by. But in this case, it was the slowest parade ever. Shyla and Ziggler weren't taking any chances; it looked like they were dragging their feet across the river bottom. Soon the water was up to Shyla's chest, but they kept moving forward.

They paused about halfway across, maybe searching the bottom for the next solid step. Then Ziggler pointed at the water in front of me. "Rees!" he called. Then, in one strong swipe of his arm, he swept Shyla to his back. She grabbed onto his hips with both hands.

I couldn't see what was in the water, but then I realized he was pointing at us, not the water.

I twisted around, only to spy a muddy black caiman about twelve feet long just behind Kat. He looked like a dinosaur on the hunt: leathery, furtive, menacing. He was approaching slowly, but as soon as his slit eyes saw my frightened ones, he charged toward us.

Kat pressed against me in a panic. I wrapped my arms around her and rolled us away from the caiman, Kat yelping as she rolled across me. We stopped in a spooning position with my back toward the caiman. I hunched my shoulders to make my neck a harder target.

Crack!

Ziggler's rifle blasted.

A dull thud followed by the sigh of a prehistoric reptile came from behind me. And then nothing but some sloppy, muddy sounds. No caiman fangs sank into my leg.

I let go of Kat. Together we hopped away from the caiman, which was writhing in the mud in jerky movements like it was being electrocuted. Its death was horrible to witness, and I thanked God Owen hadn't suffered the same way.

Your buddy just killed a real Nochedrilo.

Ziggler was still standing in the middle of the river, rifle poised to let off another round. He lowered the gun. He and Shyla finished crossing the river and he came to examine his kill. By then the caiman had stopped twitching.

"That was quite a shot. You military?" I asked.

"No, but my dad was. And he was one of those off-the-grid guys who couldn't fit back in society. I grew up in Montana living off the land. Been a shooter my whole life." Ziggler gently poked the dead caiman with the rifle. "I've bulls-eyed coyotes and bucks from a lot farther back on the ranch."

"What about that tackle in the jungle? No special training?" I asked.

"D-3 college football and a lot of luck," Ziggler said. "Now, come on. This is dinner."

My expression likely mirrored the horrified looks Kat and Shyla were giving Ziggler.

"You have a knife in that backpack?" Ziggler asked.

I didn't. A little scalpel was it, and it wouldn't stay sharp for more than an inch through the caiman's leathery skin.

Under Ziggler's direction, we turned the beast over. It must have weighed five hundred pounds. I grabbed its neck and saw where Ziggler's shot had entered.

Good thing he's on your side.

Once it was flipped, Ziggler motioned for us to back away. He lifted the rifle. "Plug your ears," he called seconds before he shot a hole in its tail. "Find me a couple sharp stones. We've got to harvest enough meat before we attract other hungry animals. We only have one bullet left."

"Why the tail?" I asked.

143

Ziggler looked at me like I was an idiot. "It's all thick meat surrounding bone. No organs. You ever clean an animal?"

My survival skills were totally different from his. He was a hunter; I was a gatherer.

Loser.

Ziggler hacked out some large chunks of tail meat and we wrapped them in leaves. "Let's get farther away before cooking this," he said as he washed his hands in the river. "I don't want every caiman crawling out of the river looking for a bite of us."

We found what seemed like a trail near where Shyla and Ziggler had come out of the river. We were about ten feet into it when Ziggler stopped at a tree with mottled light gray and army green bark. It bore a three-inch nearly horizontal slash across it.. "Someone blazed this tree with a machete. It must mark a trail."

Only a human could have made that slash. A hard, dark red globule clung to its lower end, looking almost like dried blood.

Dragon's Blood.

"Sangre de Drago," I whispered.

The others looked at me. I pointed at the sap. "A woman at the market in Tarapoto told me all about it." I'd investigated Sangre de Drago online while we were still in Tarapoto. It wasn't just snake-oil; scientists had studied the tree's sap and found it had antimicrobial and anti-inflammatory properties. There'd even been a placebo-controlled study done on humans to assess its wound-healing properties. "We should cover our wounds with it," I said.

Ziggler shook his head. "One evening on the Internet doesn't make you an Amazonian shaman."

Shyla reached to collect some. "If Rees is willing to use it, that's good enough for me."

Kat backtracked down the trail and returned with a fist-sized jagged rock, wet from her washing it off in the river. She must have been under the illusion that something hygienic was about to take place.

I struck the tree, making a little dent. I rapped harder.

Now you know what it was like to be a Neanderthal.

After a couple more whacks, dark red sap welled in the gouge.

"Cool, the tree is bleeding," Kat said, reaching out a tentative finger.

I covered a gash along my arm with a thin layer, and the sap dried quickly into a thin maroon latex. I gathered up more on my finger for Shyla's neck.

Ziggler sat back and watched, a smirk on his face as I got a good coat along Shyla's neck wound. It was like red skin glue.

Shyla didn't even wince while Ziggler looked on. "Just put some on your leg," she urged. "It's not like you're going to turn into a zombie."

Ziggler sighed. "Well, if we're going to die of Dragon's Blood poisoning, at least we all go down together." He pulled up his pant leg, exposing his gunshot wound. The bandage had already loosened and the antibiotic ointment had all washed away. Dragon's Blood had to be better than nothing.

I loaded up another finger and coated Ziggler's wound. "You're doing better than I thought."

"I think it's just a low-caliber bullet stuck in my tibia," he said like it was nothing.

Kat dabbed a little on some minor scrapes and bug bites. Then she approached me with a glob on her finger and reached up toward my face.

I ducked away.

"For your ear," she said.

"My ear?" I asked.

"You do know you're missing a chunk off the top, right?"

I felt my ear gently. I was. I remembered the sting I felt as I'd run from the church. A bullet had gotten that close to me.

We dodged death!

I stood still as Kat smoothed sap on my ear. She had a soft touch. My chest welled with excitement. For just a moment, I was an invincible warrior being anointed by a princess.

We left the tree and moved down the trail just as dusk settled in, making the jungle a bit spooky. We found a spot that seemed as good as any to make camp, about twenty feet off the trail with the hope of keeping ourselves hidden.

I pulled the shower curtain from my bag and unrolled it. The matches and the candle were still dry inside their baggie. A small victory, at least. We'd hang the other clothes around the fire to dry. But Ziggler insisted we wait until night fell before starting one so the smoke would be shrouded by darkness.

"Speak up if you have any camping tips," I said as I continued inventorying the contents of the backpack.

"Kat and I will clear an area. We can make a bed in it out of a thick layer of leaves," Shyla said.

They got to work while Ziggler and I gathered wood for a fire. Dry wood wasn't easy to come by, but I did find some branches with bark that peeled off easily to reveal drier wood underneath.

The sky darkened from gray to midnight blue to almost black. I lit the candle and used it to start a fire. Soon we had a good enough blaze to dry off completely. I handed out the extra clothes.

"We can use the shower curtain as an additional blanket if we need it," I said.

Shyla squinted. "It's a bit small for all of us."

"We won't all be under it at once," I said. "We should take turns keeping watch. But you should have something over you to keep the bugs off."

My proposal was met with silent agreement.

Ziggler skewered chunks of caiman meat on sticks, which we grilled over the fire. It might have been my hunger, but the meat was actually good.

Tastes like chicken.

Shyla handed Kat a second skewer. "If Owen were here, we'd be having our debrief about tomorrow's cases."

"*Any concerns about walking all day tomorrow, Rees?*" Ziggler mimicked in Owen's tight posture as he adjusted imaginary glasses. "*Are your flip-flops tip top?*"

I licked meat juice off my fingers. "If Owen were here, he'd be making crude jokes about eating caiman. Like that's the only way

Ziggler would get some tail."

Shyla clapped. "That's just what he'd say!"

We ate all the meat. I offered to go back and cut more we could smoke overnight, but the others thought it was too dangerous. By now, other animals—caiman or jaguars—were probably eating the carcass. And just having extra meat around the campsite could attract creatures in the night.

We tried to talk plans, but there wasn't anything to plan other than walking to Tarapoto. And in the end, our fatigue took over, so the others prepared for bed. I was taking first watch.

Kat turned to look at Ziggler in the firelight. "This has been the worst of days. Owen would end it with an amusing story. You knew him well, don't you have a story?" Her voice carried a desperation that meant this was more than just a simple request. Someone had to give the patient the medicine she needed, *stat*. And that medicine was laughter.

Ziggler paused. "This isn't an Owen story, but he loved it. A few months before the divorce, my son, Trevor, came home from school." Ziggler started to giggle just thinking of his story. Maybe Owen's plan to get Ziggler back to his old self had worked.

Ziggler suppressed a snicker and continued. "Trevor announced his science class was going to dissect 'she parts,' and that the teacher wanted the kids to run it by their parents first."

"She parts?" Shyla asked.

"I thought it was the teacher's euphemism for a woman's reproductive organs," Ziggler answered. "She parts and man bits. They were starting to learn about that stuff."

Kat gave a little giggle of her own. "Man bits," she repeated.

"Oh no, there's more," Ziggler said. "My wife immediately says, 'I'm fine with that.' But I say, 'Not so fast,' and in my mind, I'm thinking Sarah immediately agreed to it just to antagonize me because she knew I wouldn't. Then Trevor says, 'It's not a big deal, Dad. My teacher showed us some, and I wasn't grossed out at all.'"

Ziggler snickered again. "At this point, I'm flabbergasted. I'm imaging a uterus and a vagina floating in an oversized jar full of formaldehyde, but the only thing I can spit out is, 'Oh?'"

Now we were all giggling, waiting for what was sure to be a good punchline.

Ziggler could hardly talk. "And Trevor says, 'Yeah, I thought they'd be pink, but they looked more purple.' I don't know what my face looked like, but Sarah says, 'Jeez, you're the surgeon. I thought you'd be excited to have him dissect a heart.'"

Kat put her hand over her mouth to silence her laughter, and Ziggler smiled at her. "That's when it sank in," he said, shaking his head. "*Sheep hearts*, not she parts."

I bent over laughing, but also found tears filling my eyes. Of course Owen had loved the story. And now I finally knew why he called Ziggler his sheep-hearted friend. Owen had barely been dead a day, and I couldn't begin to imagine life back at the hospital without him.

As the others settled in to try to sleep near the fire, I found myself a place to perch for a few hours to listen for danger. Danger that could come from nature, from Nochedrilo...from both. Were we all just laughing like lunatics as our ship sank into the sea?

Chapter 18

I lost track of time sitting there on watch. Even after a day of running from bad guys followed by walking nonstop through the jungle, I had no problem staying awake. The memory of watching Owen die played over and over in my head.

The jungle's chirps and creaks and faint screeches, along with Ziggler's light snores, kept me on edge. Everything around me was alive in a way the Sierras weren't.

The fire's glow softened and bits of moonlight drizzled through the rainforest canopy. I found a gap between the trees large enough to glimpse a patch of night sprinkled with stars. There was a whole universe out there and I was just a speck, so much smaller than any of those tiny stars dotting the sky. One of those distant stars had a planet orbiting it. A planet with life. A benevolent life. Smart and altruistic. A planet with no need for guns or murder. A place that would view earthlings as the monsters we are.

"You think we're going to get out of here?" Kat asked from behind me.

I turned to face her. Her eyes picked up the little bit of light, but the rest of her body was camouflaged by the night. She curled her arms around her. "What if Nochedrilo is sitting waiting for us?"

I waved her to me. "I think it's just as likely that when he wakes up in the morning, his wife will tell him to give it up. She'll make him understand we were only trying to help his baby, and he'll go back to tormenting the locals instead of us."

Kat sat next to me. "Boy, you're an optimist. I hope you're right, because if I die out here, I'm going to feel like I wasted a lot of my time. I shouldn't have spent so much time being *crazy*."

"I don't think you're crazy," I said.

"You're right. You know I didn't even pee my pants? I spilled water on myself . . . by accident. A photographer caught me walking to the bathroom. He laughed and said it looked like I'd an accident. I played along and said I'd been so excited, I'd peed. He chose to ignore that I was making a joke and ran the quote like it was true."

I let Kat keep talking.

"The whole thing's a game. The real me doesn't sell records. The obnoxious me does."

She has a Lou, too!

"I'd like to know the real you," I said.

"If we get out of here..." she said.

My eyes locked on hers. "We will." There was just enough moonlight to make her eyes sparkle. And somehow, despite the rain, the mud, and the hours of walking, she still had a faint smell of cherry blossoms.

Kat leaned in for a kiss. "You're one of the good guys."

As soon as our lips touched, I heard a branch snap. I froze.

Kiss her, you idiot! This might be your last night on earth . . . kiss her!

I waited just another second in silence before I leaned forward into the kiss, but Kat was already pulling away.

Her eyes opened wide just inches from mine. She cocked her head to the side. "That tree would have given me a better smooch," she said.

"Sorry," I said. "Thought I heard something."

Dude, stop talking.

"Let's try that again," I whispered as I leaned in towards her.

This time, just as our lips planted there was a loud crunch of a footstep. Kat stopped stiff.

"Hey, Rees?" Shyla whispered loudly. "Is Kat with you?"

"Yes," Kat answered as she scooted away from me.

"I can't sleep," Shyla said.

Kat reached over and gave my hand a little squeeze as Shyla sat down next to us. "Maybe you should go get some sleep, Rees. We can take over the watch."

Oh yeah, like you'll be able to sleep after smoochus interruptus.

***

The next morning started out tough. The fitful sleep and uncomfortable bed denied any of us overnight recuperation. Joints creaked. Muscles throbbed. When Shyla suggested we take a few minutes to stretch, no one resisted.

Starting the day off with a stretch cruelly reminded me I wasn't young anymore. Ten years ago, I could've had my legs ripped off and sewn back on and then sprung up the next morning to run a marathon. But as I approached thirty-five, things just didn't heal the same. My butt ached just standing up.

There wasn't any debate about eating the last of the passion fruit for breakfast. We were optimistic we'd find other food, maybe even civilization, before day's end. And we expected rain to refill our water bottles. A day of high hopes ahead.

"I was thinking about the river we crossed yesterday," Shyla said. "I don't remember crossing a river to get to the town."

She paused as the four of us gave it thought. Five of us, counting Lou.

Damn it, we must be headed too far north. We didn't hit the road, which should have been south of us. If we're going west, it must be northwest.

The morning sunbeams shone though the canopy on an oblique angle. I held my right hand up in a beam of light and watched where the shadow hit the ground.

"Are we lost?" Kat asked.

"We might not know where we are, but we know which direction we're going," I said.

"So we're lost." Kat's voice raised an octave.

Ziggler mimicked my action just to confirm. "We're headed west."

"But what about the river?" Shyla asked.

Kat clapped her hands together. "There's got to be a loop." She outlined a letter "U" with her index finger.

She's good.

"Or it ends in a lake before hitting the road. Either way, it doesn't mean we're off track," I said.

"We just don't know where we are," Kat said with a smile.

"Okay, just tell me we're going to get out of here," Shyla said.

"We're going to get out of here," Kat said, putting an arm around her sister. She turned over Shyla's shoulder and gave me a long look, quietly questioning my confidence that we were still headed the right direction.

I gave her a firm nod. Stick to the plan. Keep moving. Westbound.

"Onward," Kat said, almost too cheerfully.

Surge on, surgeon.

In a few hours, our pace slowed as spirits dampened and the puns hit rock bottom. Ziggler stuck to the back of the group, his limp becoming more pronounced as the morning wore on.

I had him stop so I could look at his leg. The area surrounding the bullet wound felt warm to the touch and had turned the reddish pink of a pomegranate. Soft tissue swelling made the overlying skin shiny and taut. He was infected. I gave him one of my antibiotic pills and offered him some morphine for pain. He refused the morphine, looked at his leg as if were someone else's, pulled his pants leg down and kept marching.

Shyla and Kat tried to play games, but they inevitably turned into games about food. And then just simple wishes.

"What's the first meal you want when we get back to Tarapoto?" Kat asked.

"I'm craving meat," Shyla said. "A big steak."

"Have you tried lomo?" Ziggler suggested. "It's grilled steak with french fries mixed with rice and a few vegetables so you feel like it's healthy."

"Sounds awesome," Kat said.

"I'm holding out for that grilled guinea pig Sister Torres promised us," I said.

This conversation isn't healthy.

And just what should we talk about?

Need some ideas? But let me remind you that Lou is short for Lewd.

Yeah, shut it. I've got this.

"Hey, Kat, when you make up a song, do you make up the words first or the music?" I asked. The question was more than a distraction from talking about food; I was genuinely interested. I'd never made up a song in my life, and I couldn't carry a tune if it came with handles.

"I've done it both ways. But lyrics usually just pop into my head," Kat said. Just talking about music put a shot of energy into her voice.

"She's being humble. She can spout off a song like that," Shyla said. "Show 'em, Kat."

"She's exaggerating." Kat blushed.

"We showed you what we do. Now it's your turn," Ziggler said. He sounded like he meant it.

"Seriously?" Kat beamed.

Ziggler nodded.

Kat took a few more steps. She clapped her hands slowly. In a pure, sweet voice, she sang:

My friends are gone and I'm wandering the jungle alone
Been walking for miles, running from a monster man,
The blackest of crocodiles, trying to get home.
The world's a jungle, let me be the leaves on your tree,
When I'm not there, I want you to feel cold without me.

"Impressive," I said.

"I think you've got your next song," Ziggler said.

The distraction helped for a little while, but ultimately hunger took over and we stopped to eat. Our meal consisted of sips of water and half a granola bar each. We were now out of water and food.

We pushed onward. The hot, sticky air reminded me of being crammed in an elevator; every breath I inhaled felt like it had just been exhaled by the person sandwiched against me.

A spate of insect bites inspired me to reapply insect repellant. I passed the bottle around for the others to use. A small cluster of flies crawled over the bloodstain on Ziggler's pant leg. He put an extra squirt of repellant on the area. I imagined it wouldn't be long before little maggots would be crawling on his pants, trying to get to the raw meat underneath. The thought made the acid in my empty stomach churn.

Half an hour later, we came across a break in the foliage along the banks of a wide, muddy river running with water the color of milky coffee. A hundred or so yards away, a long wooden canoe carrying two men and a stack of wood crates slowly motored downstream.

"We're saved!" Kat said.

We watched them for a few seconds. The boat was skinny and the crates were stacked about five feet high. Nochedrilo probably wouldn't send a cargo canoe after us. If we let them go, it might be a long time before we saw anyone else.

I looked at Ziggler and he shrugged.

"Over here!" I yelled.

The canoe kept going. Maybe the boaters couldn't hear me over their motor. Kat and Shyla started screaming and whistling.

The boat turned abruptly toward us.

Kat high-fived Shyla. Ziggler and I smiled at each other. Finally, a way home.

The canoe didn't have much space. Wood crates filled the front half. One man was steering at the back of the boat and another stood directly behind the boxes—but they weren't boxes; they looked more like cube-shaped birdcages. There were birds in those cages.

The standing man gave a little wave and then looked down. His concentration was on something in his hands.

"I have a bad feeling about this," Ziggler said. He reached for Shyla's shirt and tugged her back a little.

As the boat got closer, the man standing behind the birdcages lifted a gun into view and took aim.

"Dive!" I yelled. I yanked at Kat as I fell back into the woods.

The two of us crashed to the ground and I rolled to her side and pushed her forward. There were a couple sharp pops from a small-caliber gun. I looked behind me but couldn't see the river, so I assumed the shooter couldn't see me, either. We lay as still as statues until we heard the whir of the motor cruise away.

Kat wriggled farther away as Ziggler and Shyla crawled toward me.

"Nochedrilo has the whole world against us," Shyla whispered.

"Naw, those guys were illegal bird catchers," Ziggler said. "They probably thought we were yelling at them for capturing the birds."

"It's the Wild West out here," I muttered.

"Ouch," Kat said as she slapped her arm. "An ant just bit me!"

Red ants swarmed everywhere.

"Yi!" Shyla swatted at one on her leg, but there were at least three others on the same calf.

A sharp sting pierced my forearm. "Yow, fire ants!" I jumped up and brushed off my arms and legs.

The four of us started dancing and swinging our arms. Ziggler slapped the back of his neck. Shyla gave her shirt a shake. Kat ran her hands up and down her legs.

"Little fuckers," Ziggler rumbled in a deeper-than-usual voice. He started twisting and writhing, trying to get to the hard-to-reach places on his back. After a few seconds of backslapping, he gave up and decided to shake his entire body while standing on his good leg, probably hoping the ants would fly off. He looked like spirits had possessed him.

We took turns slapping at each other's backs. Then, we waited only a minute before venturing back to the edge of the river. The boat motor was already out of earshot.

"We either wait for another boat or cross," I said.

"The water's calm today," Shyla said, casting her vote.

The slow-moving, murky river spooked me in its own way. Snakes, caiman, and who knows what else lurked in that water. I'd seen a child's drawing of an *anguila* on the board with all the other animals. It was a snake, or maybe an eel, in the water. I didn't know enough Spanish to understand it, but I knew enough to know ignorance wasn't bliss.

A fire ant bite on my ankle stung. I massaged it. On the bright side, a swim in the river might soothe the burn.

"Do we just walk across again?" Kat asked. She rolled up her pants legs. "Shoes on?"

"I guess so," I said. Falling in was so much easier, no choices.

"What about piranhas?" Shyla asked. She pointed to her neck and then Ziggler's leg.

"We did it yesterday," Kat said.

"But that was next to a waterfall. We'll be the only things moving in this water," Ziggler said.

Just imagine all the thrashing and pain. They could tear off all your skin and muscles and you'd still be alive. Absolute fucking torture. At least Nochedrilo would just plug a bullet in your head.

"Have you ever heard of piranhas eating a person?" I asked.

The group exchanged glances but remained silent.

"It doesn't happen," I said. "Their voraciousness is folklore. The piranhas-eating-a-cow-in-a-minute thing was rigged to impress Theodore Roosevelt. The real story is that the locals netted off part of the river and filled it with piranhas and then they starved them for a couple days. When the president arrived, they threw in a cow that had been cut open, and the piranhas attacked."

Ziggler shrugged. "They can smell blood and sense movement. That part's true. And maybe they're famished today."

"Okay, fine, you can all sit on my shoulders," I said.

They're tired, hungry, and scared. Suck it up and lead the group. It'll be just another of your stupid endurance tests to prove your manhood or something.

Lou was right. I had done a number of long hikes, run a marathon, done a century ride on my bike, all just to do it. And some were stupid, like not eating for two days just to see if I could. It wasn't about proving manliness, though. It was more about seeing what I was capable of.

I marched into the water. My feet sank into the muddy riverbed, but as soon as I got in up to my knees, I put the backpack on my chest and laid flat on my back into the water. I did a lazy backstroke.

"It's deep enough to swim," I said. "C'mon."

The others waded in.

Now's your chance to start screaming and flailing and yell "Piranhas" as you let yourself sink under the water.

It seemed Lou somehow gained strength the weaker I got. He was more vocal than ever. I disregarded his antics and kept swimming.

We were about halfway across the river when Ziggler said, "Did you see that?" He was on his back pointing downstream.

"What?" Shyla asked through a grimace of fear. She whipped her head back and forth, scouting the river.

"Something big and bumpy stuck out of the water and then went back under," Ziggler said.

"Just keep swimming," I said, picking up the pace.

"Oh my God, there are two!" Shyla yelled.

"Two what?" Kat asked, whipping her head around.

I scanned the river but didn't see anything except the rippling of the water.

"Something with a bumpy, humped back. Something big," Shyla whispered.

Bumpy? It didn't sound like a snake. Caiman? Maybe. Never again! Never would I go anywhere on a whim. Not without plenty of research first.

Kat pointed. "Look!"

This time I saw a pinkish-gray smooth bump poking up out of the water, and there was a bump on the creature's backside as it went under again. The skin was smooth and shiny with hints of pink. It looked almost like . . .

"Dolphins!" Kat exclaimed.

"Dolphins?" Ziggler repeated.

"Let's get out of here," Shyla said. "I don't think that's a dolphin. This isn't the ocean."

"No, really. The classroom had those pictures of animals. One of them was a *delfin*. There are dolphins in the river," Kat said.

"But this is freshwater," Ziggler said.

More research, I thought.

One of the dolphins did a full jump about fifteen feet away. Its stubby snout looked like a dolphin's, but it was pinker and bumpier than any dolphin I'd ever seen. The animal had to be about five feet long. I had no idea something so big could live in such muddy water.

"See, it's a good omen," Kat said. "Dolphins mean safe travel."

Ziggler moaned, "Hippy shit."

"Sailor shit," Kat shot back with a smile.

We reached the other side of the river and continued on into the shelter of the trees to rest for a moment. Almost immediately, the leaves started to patter with the sound of raindrops. When the droplets picked up to a light drizzle, Shyla pulled the water bottles out of my backpack so we could refill them.

But instead of using big leaves as funnels, we went back to the river edge to escape the trees' shelter. Shyla unrolled the shower curtain and gave us each a corner. Now the drizzle had picked up to a downpour. Within seconds, the curtain was cleaned of debris. Shyla pulled one edge down to create a spout to fill the bottles. As each was filled, she passed it around for us to drink.

We drank until we couldn't drink anymore and then refilled both bottles. I helped Ziggler use one to wash off his leg. The inflammation around the bullet wound was creeping farther down his shin and around to his calf—a bright pink warning that bacteria had found a home and were trying to claim more territory. Our situation prevented Ziggler from resting or elevating the wound. Two strikes against healing. Hopefully, the antibiotics would work. We'd know soon.

On the bright side, Shyla's neck looked great when she washed it off. Necks heal so much faster than shins. The blood of the dragon and the blood of a young woman were working together.

We took turns putting our heads under the improvised spout of water to wash our faces. I was soaking, hot, and humid, but somehow felt clean and refreshed.

Shower curtain back in my pack, we moved on through the lush undergrowth. The trail, if it could be called that, was narrower and more overgrown than the one we'd followed the day before. Were we still going the right way? Maybe the trail nearest Urycu was biggest just because that's how people entered the jungle to hunt or gather. Who would be dumb enough to walk to Tarapoto?

Just keep going. The people who get out are the ones who never stop. And look on the bright side.

Bright side?

Thanks to deforestation, you have a lot less jungle to get lost in.

An itchy red stripe flared across my right bicep. I must have brushed against something that didn't like to be touched. I resisted scratching it with my hands because I didn't want to spread the itch to other parts of my body. But soon it was more maddening than Lou, so I rubbed the arm against the bark of a tree. I kept an eye out for another Dragon's Blood tree.

The rain tapered off and quit altogether. The day had gotten its big cry out of its system and was ready to steam us again. We reapplied insect repellant as the sun burned the clouds away, confident it wouldn't be washed off seconds later in a random deluge.

Hooting and screeching noises called out from the trees ahead of us. The cacophony continued almost nonstop for a couple minutes. We approached cautiously. Some leaves in the canopy rustled. Then some others farther away waved sharply.

"Spider monkeys," I said, leading the group closer to the commotion.

The monkeys screeched and howled as they jumped from tree to tree above us. They were mostly black figures with long arms and legs and tails moving between branches.

Something flew past me and hit the ground.

"He threw a chunk of fruit at us!" Shyla said.

Fruit!

"We can eat that," I said. "Monkeys don't eat poisonous food."

Shyla looked at me like I was crazy, but Ziggler picked up a soft, yellow fruit with about a third of it nibbled away. He wiped off the outside with his wet shirt and then tore the fruit apart. He took a bite out of the freshly torn edge, avoiding the bitten part riddled with monkey germs.

Shyla and Kat looked on with wide eyes. He chewed it thoughtfully and then nodded.

"It tastes a bit like caramel custard," he said. He tore a chunk off and handed it to Kat.

Custard? Forget it, then. Let's hold out for something better.

I turned and surveyed the trees. A few fruits swayed on branches high out of reach. I wished I had the ability to swing through trees.

No way was I going to try to climb these slender trees without a prehensile tail.

So I did the next best thing and started howling at the monkeys. I ran underneath them, waving my arms in the air. "Heee, heee, waah, wah, waaah," I screeched.

There was a roar of screeches from the canopy and then a fruit flew in my direction. I picked it up. It was only half-eaten, which meant I'd just scored half a fruit!

Shyla and Kat caught on and were soon hooting and hollering at other monkeys until they threw fruits at us, too, before retreating to a neighboring tree. Soon we had some smaller, thicker-skinned red fruits. We gathered whatever fruits the monkeys had thrown as long as they showed bite marks. The tree with the smaller fruit even had a few branches low enough for us to harvest our own, unbitten fruit. We owed the monkeys lunch, and maybe dinner.

We continued along the trail. The ground was mushy where it was hilly, but the lower areas had turned to mud. "Keep an eye out for spiders and snakes," I warned. "The ground dwellers take a slightly higher position when the ground is too wet." This was definitely true for scorpions—a critter I'd encountered on other adventures.

About an hour later, Kat found a large, hairy spider perched on the bottom of a tree trunk at the edge of the path. "Too bad it's hairy. Otherwise I'd eat it," she said.

We stopped for a break on a patch of solid ground uphill from the trail. Shyla gave it her spider-free guarantee, and we sat for a rest. I laid out the shower curtain for Ziggler to lie on top of, and he propped his leg up on a log.

The longer we sat in silence, the more the world around us came alive. Birds of all sorts called out. Branches shifted overhead under the weight of unseen animals. I didn't see any more monkeys, but something was up there. A giant walking stick with impossibly long, knobby legs crawled along a branch. It was like a creature in a Salvador Dali painting.

I pointed it out to Kat and she smiled at me, longer than

necessary. That warmed me. I'd been hesitant to say anything to her all day—well, anything I really wanted to say—because we had constant company. I'd settle for a smile.

Shyla noticed us watching the insect. "What is that?" she whispered as if it might hear her and invite itself over.

"A walking stick," Kat said.

Shyla stuck her tongue out at it. "It's disgusting. It should stick to walking somewhere else."

That made Ziggler chuckle. Otherwise, he looked a little pale and a lot exhausted. I hesitated to get the group moving because his eyelids looked so heavy. A few minutes later, he fell asleep.

I'd give him a half hour or so. The three of us stayed awake, just sitting, resting. I daydreamed of home. I daydreamed of real food.

Then the rainforest fell silent as if a switch had been flipped. Kat and Shyla noticed it too. I held my index finger up to my lips. When hiking, that usually meant a predator was around.

Or a human.

There was movement from the direction of the trail ahead of us. I nudged Ziggler. He opened one eye to see me holding the gun in one hand and a finger to my mouth.

He mouthed, "What?"

I pointed in the direction of the noise, and he sat up. He took the gun from me and shifted his position so he could aim straight at the trail.

I heard a man's voice but couldn't make out what he was saying.

Ziggler held out a flat right hand and lowered it. We obeyed the command with our bodies.

The voice got louder. A second voice answered.

I could hear footsteps, and branches being pushed out of the way. Would they discover that our trail had ended here?

I spied one of the men's faces through the brush, instantly recognizing him as one of Nochedrilo's men from the previous morning. The second man I didn't recognize at all. They paused just past us, sunlight glinting off a rifle slung across the second man's back.

161

The four of us looked at each other. Kat and Shyla mirrored my worry. Ziggler's forehead was sweating. He had both hands on the gun, right thumb ready to flick the safety off and index finger poised to pull the trigger.

In what seemed like an eternity, the first man lit a cigarette and took a drag. Then they both moved farther down the trail. We waited until their footsteps faded and the birds resumed their conversation.

"They came from ahead of us," Kat said. "The road can't be far away."

"Not more than a day," Ziggler agreed.

I resisted itching my arm again as I looked in the direction the men had gone. "Once they see our tracks, they'll come back for us."

Ziggler got up with a renewed confident energy, probably be short-lived. "We've got a couple hours before dark. Let's cover some ground."

I still had my doubts. Nochedrilo's men were hunting us, and we were headed in the same direction they'd just come from.

Chapter 19

We walked until dusk. This time, we cleared a sleeping area even farther from the trail. I left the others behind to find firewood while they made camp.

I was scared to forage near the trail, so I ventured deeper into the jungle. I found a couple branches that I broke and put into my backpack. But I needed more.

While I was peering along the ground underneath large leaves, I saw a little blue-and-black-striped frog. The blue was bright, almost fluorescent, and the frog was sleek.

A poison dart frog.

A friend of mine had kept one as a pet when I was a kid. I remembered a few factoids about these deadly creatures. First, it makes its poison from what it eats, which is why frogs fed an American diet aren't poisonous. Second, its poison is one of the most deadly known to man. An amount equivalent to a couple grains of salt can kill a person. Third, its name comes from the fact that Amazonian natives would use its poison on blow-dart tips to kill prey.

I looked at my hands. Other than little bits of mud and bark from collecting wood, they were pretty clean. No cuts. Which brings me to the fourth factoid: their poison is ineffective until it gets past the outer layers of skin.

I reached down and plucked the frog off its leaf. It didn't even try to jump away. Completely docile, just like my friend's frog had been—secure in knowing it was so deadly no one would mess with it.

I dumped some of my medical supplies out of their baggie and directly into my bag. "I'm sorry, Mr. Frog, but we might need you," I said as I put the frog into the plastic bag, sealed it, and asked Mother Nature to forgive me for my next action. I used a small branch to squish the frog against a tree trunk. That ended its life.

I rubbed my palm on the ground to wipe off any poison before gathering more wood. When I returned to camp, we waited until dark and then made a fire just like the night before. I washed my hands with a bit of the water to remove any residual poison. Then we ate our fruit and drank our water in silence. No jokes tonight. Yesterday had been filled with horror and hope. Today, fatigue had eroded our hope.

Ziggler's leg looked worse. He took his antibiotics, then finally agreed to take the morphine only after I showed him I could pick up the rifle, turn off the safety, and take aim in one smooth motion.

As soon as Ziggler fell asleep, the three of us agreed we'd split the watch among ourselves so he could rest. Shyla offered to take first watch.

I flopped down next to Kat. Ziggler lay on her far side. It was maddening to have her so close to me. I rolled onto my side with my back to her. She moved into the same position. We were almost spoons. She was so close that her deeper breaths kissed the back of my neck when she exhaled. After a few minutes, she reached her left hand up to my shoulder.

Hey, buddy, are you having a heart attack? This thing's beating like a machine gun.

I put my right hand next to hers, and she grabbed it and gave it a squeeze.

I wanted to turn around and give her a kiss and a giant hug. But I didn't.

The next thing I knew I was being nudged awake.

"What?" I asked.

"Your turn," Kat said.

I sat up. Shyla was sleeping next to Ziggler on my left. The night was black beyond the weak glow of our fire.

Kat led me away from the fire. "There's a good spot to sit right over here. It's a bit in the smoke, but that keeps the mosquitoes away."

"Who's Lou?" she asked as I settled in on the log she pointed to.

"What?"

"When I tried to wake you, you said, 'quit it, Lou.'"

I paused. "Um..."

Go ahead. I dare you.

Might as well. My middle-of-the-night judgment might not be as

164

good as at other times.

"He's a voice in my head. An invisible friend of sorts," I said.

Kat pursed her lips. "Hmmf. That wasn't what I was expecting. And this friend has been talking to you your whole life?"

"Just since med school," I said. "It's a long story."

"I'm not going anywhere . . . at least until I know you're awake," Kat said.

"I watched a pregnant lady with airway swelling die during my third year. Well, not quite die. She ended up brain-dead because the anesthesiologist couldn't get her intubated in time. I'd told the OB resident she needed a surgical airway, but the resident told me it wasn't her problem. She had the baby out by emergency C-section before the mom ever got an airway. I tried to help the anesthesiologist, but I was just a med student. He dismissed me with a wave of his hand while he kept trying the same thing over and over. It didn't work."

I paused, trying to shake the memory from my head. Kat just sat quietly, listening as I continued. "Once it was obvious the mom was brain-dead, the attending OB showed up and said, 'It's not like she was a Harvard grad, anyway. The baby's safe.'"

Kat gasped, and I nodded. "That's the moment Lou showed up and said, '*Horseshit*.' Ever since then, he's been calling horseshit whenever he sees it. He harasses me, but he doesn't let things slip, from me or anyone else, and . . . well, I've said enough." I looked down, not wanting to see Kat's reaction to my deepest secret.

Kat tilted my chin back up and looked in my eyes. "As long as the voices are on your side, I don't think its schizophrenia."

See, I'm not crazy.

She rubbed the top of my head, gave me a smile, and then went off to sleep next to her sister.

Chapter 20

The next morning, we drank some water and shared the last couple pieces of fruit before getting back on the trail. A few broken branches here and there were the only evidence Nochedrilo's two men had come this way.

We didn't find any fruit trees or monkeys. No rivers, either. Just hours of jungle walk repeating over and over.

Ziggler's leg was red from the lower part of his knee down almost to his ankle. The bright red skin dimpled when I pushed my thumb against it, but I didn't feel any pus underneath. He didn't have an abscess, but he did have cellulitis, an infection of the fat and soft tissue underneath the surface of the skin. He took a double dose of the antibiotic.

In the thinner areas of the jungle, Kat and Shyla led the way. I found a large stick Ziggler could use as a crutch, and I carried the gun.

Sometime around midday, Shyla pushed her way forward past a small bush and onto a dirt road. We spilled out onto the road with excitement. Ziggler plopped onto the shaded ground at the road's edge and held up his arm. "Let's stay back a sec and figure out what to do."

"This is the dirt road, not the narrow, rutted one," I said. "If it's the one we drove in on, we might be closer to Tarapoto than I thought."

The observation lit up Shyla and Kat. Ziggler nodded like he'd had the same thought. I took out my phone and turned it on. Still no signal.

Our plan was simple: walk in the jungle alongside the road as much as possible and wave down any vehicle big enough to give all four of us a ride to Tarapoto. We didn't even see a car for the first hour. But that didn't squelch my feeling of success. I'd taken many long hikes on my own over the years, some that had lasted days. Even though I cherished nature, I also felt the warm welcome of finding a well-worn path near the end of the journey. The road served as a reminder there was more to the world than a rough jungle crawling

166

with cocaleros out to kill us.

We stayed hidden when a pickup truck going the wrong direction approached. I started doing the math. The truck ride to the village had taken a good seven hours, averaging maybe twenty miles an hour. That was a minimum of 140 miles. I had no idea how far we'd walked the day before. The road was curvy but the trail we'd hiked was straight, so it cut some mileage off. But we could still have seventy miles to go. Without food.

You'd best keep those cheerful thoughts to yourself.

In the areas where the brush was thick or the road curved, we allowed ourselves to use the road. We welcomed it for what it was—a wide-open path, no mud to sink in, no branches to push out of the way, and less bugs. But using it left us exposed to Nochedrilo. And to the sun. The jungle was hot and muggy; the road was hotter and muggier. My cheeks and ears radiated heat of their own—a sunburn was setting in. For someone who made a good chunk of my living treating skin cancer, I felt foolish without sunscreen and a hat.

Never mind a compass, food, or a helicopter.

We finished our water by noon. And the dusty heat of the road dehydrated us faster than the jungle would have.

It's rare to know thirst. Even when California is in drought, there's always water available. Faucets are everywhere. Except the Amazon.

Sticky saliva coated the roof of my mouth like rubber cement. I tried to lick my burning lower lip, but my tongue simply stuck to it. I reached up and rolled my upper lip in so it stuck to my teeth. I turned to Kat and cleared my throat. Her greasy hair hung in clumps. Her face sagged with exhaustion. She gave me a blank look.

I grinned. "Let me show you something," I snapped.

She noticed my tucked lip and realized I was playing a character. "Fire Marshall Bill?"

I chattered my teeth at her.

"He never seems to have any water when he needs it either," Kat said.

I pointed at the sky. "It's on its way."

Clouds crept along slowly. It took another hour before they covered the sun. The four of us took glances upward as we dragged along in silence, waiting for the inevitable. When it finally started to pour, we danced in the road. I felt like a sponge soaking up water. We did what we could to wash our faces and clothes. But most of all, we drank every drop we could hold, and then filled our water bottles again.

We picked up our pace. For not having any calories, the water invigorated us. The rain let up, but the clouds stayed dark with the hint that refill was soon on the way.

"Hey! You hear that?" Ziggler said.

A deep, throaty engine rumbled behind us. Ziggler and I exchanged looks. Nochedrilo drove a truck. We crouched in the bushes alongside the road, ready to jump, *hoping* to jump, but fearing the worst.

The engine kept getting louder, but the truck still wasn't in sight. Kat whispered behind me, "Even if it's Nochedrilo, I think we could take him." She put her hand on my upper back.

Her touch sparked my sense of immortality. I'd run and jump, and with a flying kick I'd tear through Nochedrilo's windshield and plant my foot into his chest. Then I'd yank him out of the truck through the broken window, and he'd beg for forgiveness as I held him up in the air by the collar of his shirt. Kat would swoon.

Don't shortchange your fantasies. What about the fireworks and the animals of the jungle all singing and holding hands?

Kat let her hand fall away as the front of the vehicle came into view.

My bravado faded. *Please don't be Nochedrilo*, I thought.

"Amazon Adventures!" Shyla said.

A short, white tour bus pulled closer. "Amazon" was spelled out across the top in green snaky letters. Just under, and partway overlapping the green letters, were blue watery letters spelling out "Adventure."

Nochedrilo didn't drive a tour bus. In unspoken unison, the four of us jumped out from the jungle and onto the road, waving our arms at the bus. The driver probably thought we were swarming with fire ants the way we danced. Ziggler planted himself in the middle of the road, giving the driver no choice but to stop.

As the bus squeaked to a halt, puzzled faces of tourists appeared in the big window behind the bus driver. Some of the faces looked disappointed to discover the things in the road ahead weren't half-naked natives, anacondas, or even monkeys. Just dirty Americans.

But we were thrilled. A tour bus wouldn't be carrying evil henchmen or cocaine growers. A few riders might snort the stuff, but none would report us to Nochedrilo.

The bus driver opened the side door. I approached it with Shyla and Kat, but Ziggler held his ground in front of the vehicle. He wasn't risking the driver closing the door and pulling away.

"Can you help us?" I asked.

"We've been stranded in the jungle for two days," Shyla added in Spanish.

A pale, gray-haired woman tourist with a woven hat and pink plastic sunglasses turned her mouth into a perfect *O* and her eyebrows into upside down *V*s. "Oh heavens," she said.

The bus driver looked Kat and Shyla up and down. "There's room in the back." He looked like he wished he could've said no.

"Are you going to Tarapoto?" Kat asked.

The driver nodded.

I waved Ziggler in.

The bus driver stopped Ziggler at the door. "No guns," he said.

Ziggler unloaded the rifle and put the bullet in his pocket. He offered the gun to the driver. "It's yours if you want it."

The driver contemplated the weapon a second and then held out his hand, tucking the rifle between his seat and the door.

It wasn't until we were on the bus that I appreciated how slimy we were. The enclosed space made our stench unavoidable. More than a few people gave us skeptical looks bordering on snobby. Others leaned toward the closest air-conditioner vent.

It was a short bus with about twenty passengers. The back couple of rows were open—the bouncy seats. But beggars can't be choosers.

And motion sickness might make you smell better.

We flopped into the seats. My body thanked me for securing a moment to relax. The bus lurched forward. Home was in sight.

I turned and looked out the window. An old woman dressed in what looked like layers of blankets was standing on the edge of the road. Her eyes caught mine. I recognized her deep wrinkles. She nodded at me.

I pressed up against the window to try to keep her in view. It was impossible. We just walked that road. There wasn't a woman on it. Where did she come from?

"So, what's your story?" A voice in front of me asked.

A meddlesome man in his mid-twenties sporting a thin goatee and black glasses peered over the back of his seat at us. His eyes rested on Kat. "Has anyone ever told you that you look like Crazy Kat?"

Kat waved her hand dismissively. "I get that a lot," she said with a light laugh.

"What happened? Where's your car?" the guy asked.

"First things first," Kat said. "What's your name?"

"Richard," he said, taken slightly aback.

"Richard, we haven't had any real food in two days and my friend has an infected leg. Do you happen to have any food or antibiotics?"

Richard pushed his glasses up with his thumb. "Uh, yeah." He clapped his hands twice and called out, "Hey, everyone. These guys haven't eaten anything since yesterday. They spent the night in the jungle. If you've got anything to eat or drink, pass it back. Anyone have any antibiotics? This guy's sick."

A few people asked for confirmation and details; others looked back with curiosity. Someone muttered, "That explains things" just loud enough for most of the bus to hear. And the others sounded like they were bored of Loud Richard.

Ziggler had sprawled across the seats behind me, back against the window and leg propped up on the seat next to him. Someone passed him a bottle of antibiotics and a banana. I watched him lodge a pill into a chunk of banana like he was going to trick a dog into eating it.

Good boy.

All I wanted was to lie back in my semi-cushioned, non-reclining chair and sleep. My body ached, and I was so tired I knew I was bordering on involuntary shutdown. But the bus driver was talking to someone on his cell phone while repeatedly checking on us in the rearview mirror. I wanted to believe he was just telling his wife about finding some filthy Americans on the road, but I'd seen too much not to worry.

Hey, his phone's working.

His phone was working! I took mine out of its plastic bag and powered it on. A little spinning icon searched for a signal. Then the screen went black and an empty battery flashed three times before the phone turned off completely. No matter, we were on the bus to Tarapato, the start of the trip home.

Loud Richard asked for more details. What exactly had happened?

Kat made up a story. "In short, we ended up in the jungle without our ride, guide, or supplies other than some matches and a blanket," she told him, and everyone else listening.

The tourists started asking each other questions. How could that have happened? How had we gotten separated from our guide? Between murmurs, they passed back granola bars, energy bars, a couple candy bars, and a few bottles of water.

I devoured a granola bar. It had coconut in it, which is usually a deal breaker, but I was so hungry my taste buds didn't put up a stink. Then I wolfed down a peanut butter energy bar. It was one of the best meals I'd ever had.

"Is that your missing guide?" Loud Richard asked. He pointed out the back window.

A black truck roared up the hill behind us.

Shyla, Kat, and Ziggler turned at the sound.

"Fuck," Ziggler grunted.

Shyla ducked behind the seat and pulled Kat down with her. "Get down," she urged Ziggler and me, her voice shaking.

"Face forward," I ordered Loud Richard as I swung sideways behind his seat. "Act like we aren't here."

But now the entire bus was looking back at the quickly approaching truck. Across the aisle, Kat and Shyla watched me, their eyes wild with fear and exhaustion.

The low grumble of the truck's engine approached and then began to pass the bus on the left. The motor growled like an angry dog. A dog about to bite.

As soon as the truck passed, I popped my head up to quickly peek out the window. What I saw was exactly what I'd feared: Nochedrilo's black truck.

Chapter 21

The truck pulled ahead of the bus and began to brake, forcing the tour bus driver to do the same until the bus slowed to a stop. We sat up in our seats. No sense in hiding now.

A few of the tourists looked back at us skeptically. A young woman a few rows ahead obviously saw the fear on Shyla's face, going pale herself while looking back and forth from the truck to us.

"If that's not your ride, then who is it?" Loud Richard asked.

"The fucking devil," Kat answered. "He killed our friend."

The whole bus seemed to hear Kat's answer and went silent.

The bus driver turned toward us. His voice trembled and he shrank back against the steering wheel like he was more afraid of us than Nochedrilo. "You need to get off. All of you."

Fear and bewilderment rippled through the passengers. Most began to guess this was a robbery of sorts. Some of them patted their pockets or hidden money belts as a reflexive check.

Too bad there wasn't a back exit to the bus; we could have run back into the jungle.

No. Sister Torres said the only way to beat Nochedrilo is to fight.

She also said anyone who loses dies.

Don't lose.

"Stall," I said. I grabbed my backpack.

Ziggler stood and plowed his way up the aisle to the front of the bus. "Give me back the gun. I'll kill him, and we can get on our way."

The bus driver shook his head. "He'll kill all of us."

Ziggler was almost on top of the bus driver but it was too late. The sound of metal rapping on glass ripped through the shell-shocked bus as Nochedrilo tapped the door's window with the tip of his gun. The driver opened the door, and Nochedrilo said something to him.

The driver gushed thank-yous while trembling with fear. Then he yelled at us again to get off the bus. Ziggler didn't move, glancing back at me.

"Just a minute," I said from behind my seat. "A full minute," I muttered to myself.

I heard Nochedrilo's voice from the front.

The bus driver cried, "He says he's going to start shooting people from the front of the bus going back if you don't get out right now."

Shrieks rippled in the air. A man yelled, "Get off the bus!" More people echoed in agreement.

Ziggler moved forward slowly, and Shyla and Kat followed. They moved like molasses down the aisle. I got up behind them, backpack in one hand and cell phone in the other. I passed the phone to Loud Richard, now uncharacteristically silent. "If I don't come back, charge my phone and call my mom."

He took the phone and nodded solemnly.

The bus driver shook his head slowly as I passed. Under his breath, he repeated, "Nochedrilo. Lo siento. Lo siento."

Yeah, real sorry.

Nochedrilo backed away from the door to let the four of us shuffle off the bus. A sick grin plastered his leathery face. As we walked by, he pointed his gun at each of our faces in turn.

Once we were off the bus, Nochedrilo pulled a wad of money out of the pocket of his black leather jacket. He peeled off a couple bills and handed them to the driver. The hand with the gun never seemed to waver no matter what the rest of his body was doing. No doubt he was a better shot than his minions.

"Tell him to let the others go," I yelled back to the bus driver. "They weren't there when his daughter died."

The bus driver froze with fear. He glanced at Nochedrilo and then slowly reached his trembling hand onto the button to close the door. Nochedrilo raised an eyebrow at him, and the driver stammered something to Nochedrilo, who then replied. "It doesn't work like that," the bus driver translated. "Sorry."

He closed the door and restarted the engine. The bus pulled backward and then stopped. I expected the driver to squeeze the bus past Nochedrilo's truck and leave us behind, but he didn't.

Fucker backed his bus up so he wouldn't get blood on it.

Shut up. You aren't helping.

The passenger door of Nochedrilo's truck stood open. Dr. Yanpa leaned against the front of the truck, watching us. When I locked eyes with him, he shifted his position and lifted one shoulder. Told you so.

Shyla began pleading with Nochedrilo in Spanish. He didn't even respond, just pointed toward the side of the road with his gun. I suspected a jungle execution.

He offered Owen a chance to fight him.

"Shyla, tell him I'll fight him," I said. "If he wins, he gets to kill all of us. If I win, we get to go. He's already killed Owen out of revenge."

"Are you crazy? Even if you win, he's still going to kill us," Shyla said.

"You're brave," Ziggler said. "If you lose, I'm next."

"You're stupid," Shyla said.

"Ditto," Kat said.

"Tell him," I repeated.

"You don't have to do this," Shyla said.

"No other choice at this point," I said. Keep moving forward.

Her lips trembled. "Nochedrilo," she called. We all stopped walking.

The doctor stepped to Nochedrilo's side with a look of indifference.

As the words were exchanged, I watched Nochedrilo's face. His first response was a chuckle. Then he sized me up with beady eyes and laughed. He glanced toward the bus. The driver was watching. He looked at the doctor. Dr. Yanpa gave him a double nod of encouragement. Shyla and Nochedrilo had a few more exchanges.

"What is it?" I asked.

"He said that if you beat him, he'll let the three of us go. But he's still going to kill you because of Jimena." Shyla's lip started to tremble. She quickly added, "But I told him that wasn't fair."

Nochedrilo and I would never come to an agreement on what was *fair*.

"Great," I said.

"What do you mean, great? He's going to kill you!" Shyla said.

"Yeah, but if I win, you three go free," I said.

"Kick his ass," Ziggler said. He held out a fist to me. I hit it.

Nochedrilo handed his gun to the doctor. The doctor played with the weight of the gun before aiming it at me.

Maybe the language barrier made this worse. If we all spoke the same language, we probably could have hashed things out.

Yeah, maybe you could teach him modern medicine.

Or maybe just make him understand we were trying our best.

Dr. Yanpa tucked the gun into his pants and then gave Nochedrilo a sharp slap on the back of the shoulder.

This was the craziest, dumbest, and bravest moment of my life. I reminded myself I didn't have an alternative. My hands started to sweat. Especially the one holding a loose 22-gauge needle that I'd just scraped across the back of a poison dart frog. The chemicals in its tiny shaft were more powerful than any punch I could throw, as long as I could get close enough to use it.

Chapter 22

Nochedrilo stepped back and motioned me forward.

Kat tapped my shoulder. When I turned, she gave me a firm kiss on the lips. A real kiss. And this time I didn't mess it up.

My adrenaline surged. The kiss was far too short. Every millisecond of it gave me more power. If her lips stayed on mine long enough, I'd be able to leap skyscrapers.

When she pulled away, she gave me a hug. Her cheek brushed against mine as she whispered in my ear, "If you kill him, we all go free."

I set the backpack on the ground. "Whatever happens, don't touch that bag," I said.

She stepped back as quickly as she'd come forward, a strange look on her face. I guessed those weren't the parting words she'd expected.

I turned to face Nochedrilo.

He beckoned to me with his right hand, giving me a close-mouthed smile. I stepped forward. I moved the needle into position between my index and middle finger, making a fist so the tip of the needle protruded from my fingers between the knuckles.

If watching martial arts movies counted for anything, I'd have nothing to worry about. But I'd only had a couple years of karate as a teenager. Some of the principles stuck, but I never heard people reference the muscle memory of karate being just like riding a bike.

I turned sideways. A narrower target is harder to hit. I put my left fist up near my shoulder, prepared to block. I cocked my loaded right fist back and lowered my stance. The bent knees and spaced feet gave me a low center of gravity and, therefore, better balance.

"It doesn't have to be like this," I said.

"Yes, it does," Nochedrilo said.

"I knew you understood English."

"Sick fuck, that was new to me." Nochedrilo smiled as he put both fists up and crouched a little. A boxer. Of course.

I glanced at his heavy boots. He might be a little less nimble in them, but a kick from them could be crippling. My hiking shoes were nothing special. If I had known I'd be in a fight to the death, I would've brought along my steel-toed boots. And Floyd Mayweather.

Nochedrilo threw a few jabs in the air for intimidation.

What an idiot.

Lou was not as terrified as me. Probably because he didn't have a body.

Hey, buddy, let me take over. I can beat this assmunch.

Why?

I don't feel pain the way you do. I don't think about things the way you do.

You're my inner pit bull?

Before Lou could answer, Nochedrilo stepped forward and threw four or five rapid punches at me. Most of them hit my left arm, but as he threw he drifted higher, making me raise my arm in defense. He stepped into his last punch and went low, hitting me in the back left on my lowermost rib.

I felt the bone shift and moan. I let out a cry but hardly heard it. My sense of hearing turned off. Some primitive brain process kicked in and decided not to devote any bandwidth to hearing. Turns out the cochlea doesn't matter much in hand-to-hand combat.

Nochedrilo stepped back, grinned, and approached again.

This time I blocked the first two punches and stepped forward to deliver a right punch into his abdomen. He moved to the side as I made contact. The needle sank into the side of his leather jacket and lodged there.

My poison dart had missed!

Nochedrilo took advantage of my pause, stepping forward to hit me in the left chest and shoulder. I jumped back in pain.

Fight! Stop thinking about the needle.

But I could see the hub sticking out of his coat. If I could hit it just right . . .

Nochedrilo approached again and threw more punches at my arm, trying to get me to raise it again. Instead, I let him hit my deltoids, and then I threw a punch straight at his face. He saw it coming, and instead of blocking it, he bowed his head and let me hit him straight on top of the forehead.

It felt like punching a brick wall. Pain exploded in my knuckles. Nochedrilo stepped back, smiling.

My blood turned to acid. I felt it burning in my temples and my fists. It singed away the pain. My knuckles no longer hurt. Neither did my ribs.

I lowered back into my stance.

Nochedrilo circled to my right. I pivoted to keep him at my side. I could see Ziggler, Kat, and Shyla watching me. It looked like Ziggler shouted something, but I couldn't hear him. As we turned a little farther, I saw the front window of the bus full of faces. A few of the tourists were taking pictures or video. They would know exactly who killed me.

Maybe Nochedrilo thought it would distract me to have the spectators in the background. Maybe he was just circling. But once we'd turned a full 180 degrees, he lunged forward to take me down with some sort of wrestling move. Instead of jumping backward, I took a lesson from Nochedrilo and drove my right knee forward to meet him.

Nochedrilo was a short guy going low. My knee collided with his face as he tried to wrap his arms around me. His nose cracked as it broke, and he let out a grunt. I leapt out of his reach. Nochedrilo fell forward onto the ground but immediately pushed himself up. A blast of blood spouted from his nose like a whale clearing its blowhole.

Nochedrilo licked the blood off his upper lip. A thick drip hung off his chin. He gave his head a shake, and then it was gone. He was no longer smiling.

He took off his coat and threw it to the side, unaware that my weapon was with it. I glanced at the coat. Just finding the needle without poking myself would take too much time. And he wasn't going to give me a second.

Nochedrilo's eyes turned to slits like an attacking shark, and he rushed forward with fists flying. The most I could do was curl up. Most of his punches hit my arms, but some of them connected so solidly I thought he was going to break bones.

Nochedrilo grunted something in Spanish with every other

punch and every now and then did a slobbery exhale. Little droplets of blood and spit hit my bare arms. For a split second, it disgusted me.

Nochedrilo spun around me and connected solidly with my ribs. A couple of them ached so sharply I wished I didn't have to breathe.

I'd never been beaten before. I'd taken a couple good hits as a kid, but those hurt more emotionally than anything else. This was a true assault.

You have to do something now. Before he breaks something important. Before he kills you.

I took a step backward into my stance, and as Nochedrilo stepped forward, I plowed toward him. I swung my right elbow up in an attempt to hit his left temple. He blocked it easily, but I took advantage of the proximity and drove my right knee into his crotch. I felt the bone of his pelvis lift off the ground. Nochedrilo dropped back with a groan.

I took a deep breath and it felt like shards of my broken ribs jabbed into my muscles. I let the air rush out of my lungs, and the pain dissipated.

Nochedrilo looked up at me, a little more green than before but still steaming. Then he stood proudly, like he had no pain. So macho. He stepped up to me again, this time more slowly. I threw a few punches in between his jabs, but couldn't get to his face. I landed a solid punch into his chest, but Nochedrilo didn't flinch; instead he returned with a barrage of punches. One of them blasted past my block into my cheek, snapping my head back. The edges of my world blackened.

Bite your tongue! Don't you dare pass out. Three other lives depend on you!

I gave the tip of my tongue a sharp snap. The pain jolted me back to full consciousness. I tasted the blood.

Fear crept into me. Real fear. The I-think-I'm-going-to-die type of fear. I had to incapacitate Nochedrilo soon, but I didn't know how. Could I land enough punches to his head to knock him out? It looked like he had a knife strapped to his belt, but the holster had one of those snaps over it. I doubted I could somehow get the knife and stab him before he pummeled me unconscious.

I can do it. Let me take over.

Don't ever give the voices control.

Fuck that. Besides, there are no voices.

Nochedrilo threw punches, one right after the other. I blocked with my left hand, swinging it back and forth. Sweep left. Sweep right. My hand hit Nochedrilo's arm just in time to turn a blow into a glance.

Nochedrilo didn't care. A few blocks didn't deter him. He kept punching like a lumberjack swinging an axe, each one hard and confident that eventually, the tree would fall.

This guy is trying to kill me because I did my job.

He must be a C-student.

I've had enough of this shit.

You swore!

Yes, we did, now what have you got?

Lou is short for Hulk.

My whole body tingled like ice water ran through my veins. Goose bumps rippled across my arms. A hot surge of adrenaline washed away the cold. Lou was somewhere inside me, wringing the last bit of hormone out of my adrenal glands. I lowered my stance and tightened my fists. The world became crisp and slow.

Sweat and blood dripped off Nochedrilo's face. A trail of blood exited his left nostril and entered his mouth. Congealed blood filled the spaces between his teeth.

I noticed that Nochedrilo's head drifted slightly toward the side of his roundhouse punch just before he threw it. One after the other.

Just as he was pulling back a left roundhouse, I skipped forward and planted my left foot on his boot. At the same time, I jabbed my left fist straight into his face. It was a weak punch, but it hit his already broken nose. The cartilage and bone shifted under the weight of my fist.

Nochedrilo looked up, stunned. He tried to step back, but my foot was still pinning his boot to the ground. I stepped forward with my right foot while delivering a second punch with my left.

Nochedrilo blocked it with his right arm. I opened my left hand and swept his arm upward just enough so my palm covered his face. At the same time, I launched a straight punch with my right.

Nochedrilo saw it coming and tried to get his left forearm up to block. But I kept my punch low, and it found a way under his arm near the elbow. My fist connected with the front of his neck. I felt the soft tissues compress against his spine. I visualized the airway cartilages crushing and breaking.

I lifted my left foot and he staggered backward. His left hand went to his throat. His breath gargled, and a look of bewilderment flashed through the anger on his face. Nochedrilo glanced at Dr. Yanpa and opened his right hand.

The gun!

Not a chance, motherfucker.

I rushed forward and blasted Nochedrilo's chest with an open-palm punch straight into his ribs. I felt one of them crack under the heel of my palm.

Nochedrilo flew backward. I followed him as he fell to the ground. He used his arms to break his fall, but I was there to drop knee-first onto his chest.

A gunshot exploded and I froze.

Dr. Yanpa pointed the gun straight up. The fight was over.

Nochedrilo stopped struggling.

"We were trying to save her," I said to him.

Dr. Yanpa motioned with the tip of the gun for me to get off his boss. I did.

Nochedrilo tried to talk, but all he could muster was a sick, bubbly *larrggle* sound. He coughed, expelling clots of blood. He sucked in another raspy breath and exhaled with a gurgle. His crushed airway was swelling shut.

Nochedrilo put his right arm up with a hand out. He surrendered. And Lou slipped back into a deep realm, leaving me to feel the pains in my bones and muscles.

Dr. Yanpa waved the gun at all of us. "Get in the bus."

"You're letting me go?" I asked.

Dr. Yanpa shrugged. "You earned it, and he's never going to know."

Shyla and Kat ran up to me, but I waved them off. The idea of being touched anywhere was too painful.

The other three climbed onto the bus first. I stepped to the door and heard a gurgle from Nochedrilo. A gasp and sucking noise. A noise I'd heard before.

The bus driver pointed at Nochedrilo. The beaten cocalero was sitting up, leaning forward, chin out, just like Mrs. Childs trying to suffocate. He, too, was going to choke to death, and Dr. Yanpa just stood there, watching.

I stepped onto the bus, ready to leave. I looked out the front window. There sat the man who'd killed Owen, who would kill me if given another chance. All I had to do was walk away, let nature take its course. It wasn't my responsibility to try to save the brutal man's life. Nochedrilo had Dr. Yanpa for that. I had my friends' lives to think about, not to mention my own.

I took another step up onto the bus. Nochedrilo deserved this miserable death. Yes, his daughter had just died, but he'd executed Owen. That wasn't revenge, it was cold-blooded murder.

First, do no harm.

My feet stopped yet again.

"Rees, hurry!" Kat screamed from the bus.

"Get over here before he changes his mind and shoots you," Ziggler bellowed.

But the words from the oath I'd committed myself to the first day I walked into medical school echoed in my head. In my heart. Throughout my broken body.

First, do no harm.

I staggered up the remaining stairs of the bus and grabbed the driver's shirt collar.

"Do you have a pen?"

Chapter 23

"Sí . . . yes," he stammered, fishing a ballpoint pen from a slot on the dashboard and handing it to me.

I backed out of the bus. When my foot planted on the ground, it sent a jolt of pain to my ribs. I definitely had broken ribs.

I hurried to Nochedrilo, pulled the pen apart, and tossed the ink aside. I pulled out the black plug at the top. I showed it to him. At this point, it was no longer a pen, just a hollow tube, one end pointier than the other.

Dr. Yanpa cleared his throat. "You just can't leave it, can you?"

I ignored him.

Nochedrilo stared at the pen, probably worried I was about to finish the job. Who knows, maybe he'd used a pen to stab someone to death. This was a guy known for cutting off fingers. Or perhaps he was worried I wasn't going to fix him before time ran out.

I pointed to the center of his neck, held the pen near my mouth, and made a sucking sound like I was breathing through it. "I'm going to make a hole in your neck, and you're going to breathe though this tube."

I reached down to his right hip and unsnapped the knife. It was a pointy, narrow knife, about four inches long. The sun lit up the edge. It looked as sharp and clean as any scalpel. It was a knife that could kill.

Or save.

I pushed Nochedrilo's shoulder to lower him to the ground. Then I pushed his chin up. The landmarks jumped out of his skinny neck. With my left index finger, I traced out the thyroid cartilage, the cricothyroid membrane—the site of an emergency airway—and then his trachea. Given the injury, I wanted to go lower than normal, but I was limited by the risk of bleeding. A knick in any of the vessels of the thyroid would be a mess.

With Nochedrilo lying down, he was hardly moving any air. I took the knife and sliced the skin overlying the membrane all the way down to the airway. He winced and let out a whimper. His left hand reflexively shot up to push me away, but he restrained himself. I slid the pen into the opening in his neck and felt it pop into the windpipe.

Nochedrilo's next breath was silent except for the slight whistle of breathing through the pen. I held it tight, sawing it in half with the knife. A shorter tube meant less air resistance.

I set the knife aside, grabbed Nochedrilo's left hand, and wrapped it around the tube. He was now in control of his airway.

"You're a better man than I am," Ziggler said from behind me. "I can think of far better uses for that knife."

I stood, and Nochedrilo sat up.

"Let's go," Ziggler said. He pulled at the back of my shirt.

I followed. I looked back at Dr. Yanpa and Nochedrilo to see them watching me go. Nochedrilo had his hand to his throat. He took a breath in and then plugged the tube with his finger. This forced his exhalation up his throat and out of his mouth. "Thank you," he said as the bus engine sputtered to life.

"Dr. Rees, get over here," Dr. Yanpa called.

"Don't go," Ziggler said.

I didn't think I had a choice. I walked over to him.

"Did Alvaro find you in the jungle?" the doctor asked.

"Yes, if he was wearing a brown vest," I said.

"Kill him?"

I nodded.

"Did you take his gun?" Dr. Yanpa asked.

"We threw it into the jungle," I replied.

Dr. Yanpa lifted his gun. "I suppose that's the gun I'll tell people you shot Nochedrilo with," he said.

"But I . . ." I started.

Nochedrilo's eyes grew wide and a guttural noise escaped around the pen.

Dr. Yanpa spun and shot Nochedrilo in the face. The blast vaporized his forehead.

When I was a teenager, my friends and I would sometimes put a firecracker in a big, juicy strawberry and watch it transform into a red spray with a *pop*. This was the sort of thing kids did in strawberry farm country. The top of Nochedrilo's head did the same thing. The ground was sprayed with red, along with chunks of brain and skull. The rest of Nochedrilo's body fell backward and thumped to the ground.

"What the . . . ?" I screamed.

Fuck.

Dr. Yanpa walked over to the body, plucked out the makeshift airway, and then threw the pen into the trees. He fired a second shot into the site of the emergency airway. Nochedrilo's body jumped from the slug's impact. His neck was now a gaping hole of bloody hamburger.

"What are you doing?" I yelled. I almost raised my hands in the air for exclamation, but my rib pain reminded me not to move too fast.

Dr. Yanpa slid the safety on Nochedrilo's gun and tucked it into his pants. "You idiot! You were supposed to beat him and LET HIM DIE. If someone kills my boss, then it's my duty to take over the business."

I just stood there, dumbfounded at the ease with which Yanpa had taken Nochedrilo's life. Just to move himself one notch up a ladder. Sick. The people of Urycu won't have much to celebrate if this psychopath filled Nochedrilo's shoes.

"But there's a whole bus of witnesses," I blurted.

"Do you think the police in Tarapoto are going to come here and set things straight? Do you think that bus driver is going to say anything?" Yanpa laughed while he plucked Nochedrilo's wallet from the dead man's pocket and helped himself to the money. He handed me a few bills. "Give this to the driver. He knows the routine."

I took the money. "But if you were going to kill him, why'd you let me save him?"

"After everything, you still can't stop yourself, you haven't learned a thing. You don't belong here. I hope your wounds remind you of that." Yanpa looked down his nose at me and twisted up the corner of his slit lips. "Now get out of here before I make you drag his body into jungle."

I wanted to say something cutting, something to make the doc realize his routine was pure evil. But instead I rephrased what Owen had told him. "A long time ago, you took an oath. You should try honoring it."

Yanpa huffed.

When I got close to the bus, I picked my backpack off the ground. I couldn't leave that behind.

"Wait," Dr. Yanpa ordered.

I looked at him.

"I keep the bag," he said. "I knew you had money with you."

"I wouldn't—"

"Shut up and give me the bag," he interrupted.

"But it's—" I tried.

Yanpa put his right hand on the gun tucked into his pants. "I don't want to hear it."

I took my passport from the top pocket. "Just keeping my passport," I said. I held it by the edge of the front cover, shaking it so he could see there weren't any bills folded between the pages.

Yanpa snatched my backpack away with his left hand, right hand still on the gun.

I backed away.

This time, when I got to the bus, the driver opened the door. I stepped aboard and made the mistake of reaching my left arm up the railing. My ribs screamed.

I slapped the money into the bus driver's hand. He shrugged. The cash disappeared into one of his pockets in a flash. The driver made eye contact with Yanpa. The doctor put an index finger to his lips and then waved his hand in a flat motion, like he was telling a blackjack dealer "No more."

The driver nodded. Then he looked at me and jerked his thumb toward the back of the bus. As I walked past, he said, "Now Nochedrilo is Dr. Nochedrilo."

Half the bus riders were pale with shock. Many of them were shaking, and some were crying. They all had looks of incomprehension, except one. "Bus driver said that guy killed your friend a couple days ago and you just won your freedom from the new boss," Loud Richard said. "Sounds pretty fucked up."

I just nodded my head. I didn't have the energy or desire to try to explain all that had happened. It wouldn't make sense to a rational person anyway.

The driver shifted the bus into gear. Chatter and whispers spread across the aisle as people tried to guess what had actually just happened.

I sank into a seat on the right side of the bus in the far back.

"You saved us," Shyla said, reaching forward to pat me on the head.

"It was a group effort," I said.

I looked out the window as the bus started moving. Yanpa held my backpack in his left hand and reached inside with his right. Then he reflexively yanked his hand back out, letting the bag fall to the ground as he held his hand up. I could see the needles sticking out of it. My needles. The poison needles I booby-trapped the backpack with. I'd tried to warn him not to take it.

Dr. Yanpa—Dr. *Nochedrilo*—started to pull the needles out, looking up and shaking a fist at me as the bus slowly passed. I turned my head, pressed my face against the window, and watched as he turned over the backpack to dump out its contents. He inspected the baggie with the frog remnants, frowning as if realizing what had happened. Then he pulled the gun out of his waistband and pointed it straight at my window as the bus began to pick up speed.

But before he could shoot, he slumped onto his knees and fell forward onto the ground next to Nochedrilo. We rounded a curve and all I could see was trees. No doctor. No Nochedrilo. Just miles and miles of trees.

Kat slipped into the seat next to me and leaned in close. "Thanks," she said, taking my hand in hers and giving me a smile.

I wanted to sweep her up in my arms and return the kiss, but as soon as I tried to move, my broken ribs called out in pain. Instead I leaned back, closed my eyes, and let Lou invent all sorts of meanings for her smile.

Chapter 24

Back in the United States, we told the authorities what had happened. A wave of interrogations and media coverage followed. The investigators found a video of me fighting Nochedrilo that one of the tourists had posted. It didn't go viral, but the exposure was enough that I understood Kat's distaste for the spotlight. For months, every patient began their visit with, "Didn't I see you in the paper?"

Shyla kept quiet at work about what had happened. I didn't think she'd ever go on another mission. Maybe Kat would have been able to talk her into it, but Shyla created a substitute here at home. She beefed up on her Spanish, and at the end of every clinic day, we now see a couple patients who don't have insurance. Most of them are Spanish-speaking day laborers.

Six months after we returned home, Ziggler won partial custody of his sons. The rumor around the hospital was that his near-death experience had made him realize how important family was. I doubted that. I think he'd always wanted to be with his sons; that's why he'd been so miserable even before the trip turned to crap. Sometimes I see him limping down the hallway on the way to the OR. He'll give me a nod or shrug, but rarely anything more.

Kat recorded another album entirely of her own making. It was a huge success, garnering nominations for awards I didn't know existed, plus a few everyone's heard of. After a short tour, she disappeared into relative obscurity. But to the people who knew her well, that meant Northern California.

About nine months after our return, I received a package from Peru. Part of me was afraid to open it. I feared Owen's eye would be in it . . . or Sister Torres's finger.

But Owen was buried. They'd brought his body back. And the bad guys were dead.

But bad guys always have more bad guy friends. Which was why I wasn't keen on ever going back to Peru.

I still hadn't opened the box by the time Kat came by my place a few hours later. "Give it to me," she said. "I'll open it." She tugged the package out of my hand and pulled at the brown paper.

Since I hadn't known Kat before the mission, it's hard for me to say how much she's changed. But she has fearlessness in her I didn't recognize at the beginning. It's like she felt like she was a passenger in life, but once she realized she was in the driver's seat, she decided to see what this thing can do.

I grabbed the package from her and opened it myself.

Kat sat on my lap as I pulled out the box for my surgical loupes, plus an envelope. I opened the box to see my loupes, a bit dirty, but nothing more. I opened the envelope and pulled out a letter and a drawing.

It was the drawing of the Nochedrilo. The black alligator looked cute, far tamer than the beast it represented.

I unfolded the note.

"Why did Sister Torres send all this?" Kat asked. "We'll be seeing her soon enough."

I harrumphed and held up the letter so both of us could read.

Dr. Rees,

I am sorry that Dr. Owen died. Through his death, you saved many people in our humble town. Please know that in one small part of the world, you are a hero. The children are no longer afraid of the monster. They thank you.

This is how the Lord works.

God Bless,

Sr. Amelia Torres

P.S. We can't wait to see you and Kat next summer. We owe you a guinea pig dinner!

I gave Kat a fake glare. "Did you tell Sister Torres we were coming next summer? I thought we were still discussing that!"

"I told you there'd be no better way to spend my last summer," Kat smiled. "Otherwise I'd have to finish med school and residency before I'd have time for a mission trip."

Kat flipped around on my lap so she was facing me. "This is a level three trip, Rees. They need our help. They don't even have Dr.

191

Yanpa to help them now."

I sighed. Owen would go back, no hesitation.

Lou used to push me to do all sorts of things I wasn't excited about. But now I was with someone who did the same. She was impossible to ignore, far more persistent, and even more successful.

That's one of the reasons I love her.

"C'mon, Urycu needs its hero," Kat pleaded, and kissed my cheek.

I smiled and nodded yes, but I didn't feel like a hero. I felt like a guy who'd just done what he had to do to survive. To protect his friends. Sometimes I wished we'd never tried to help Jimena at all. Maybe then Owen would still be alive.

But whenever I had that thought, another immediately followed. I wasn't sure if it was my voice or Lou's; I can't really tell them apart anymore. But the voice spoke loud and clear.

Fuck that kind of thinking. Don't ever be ashamed for trying your best.

THE END

ACKNOWLEDGMENTS

Thanks to the usual cast of characters for their help, constructive criticism, ideas, and unconditional friendship. Ange McQuade almost deserves credit on the front cover of the book. Cohan Andersen could have watched more than a few bad movies with the time he put into this literary endeavor. Laine and Katy (Sprinkel) Morreau both made the novel more readable and fun to look at.

I have a debt of gratitude to all the patients who serve as inspiration and learning experiences. I'm sorry so many parts of this book are true. I wish I could cure you all. And thanks to the doctors, nurses, and medical assistants who help me help others.

Last, but not least, thanks to Vivian. This book doesn't have any tortured geishas in it, so you probably won't read it, but I love you anyway. Thanks for your constant encouragement.

I'd be remiss to not acknowledge Zeppelin and Jinx. Thanks for so many hours nestled by my feet while I typed. Since you aren't literate, I'll make up for it with an extra rawhide bone.

Thanks to you, reader, for joining me on my adventures. If you enjoyed the ride, please tell others about it. If you didn't then don't tell anyone.

Hope to see you again sometime soon.

ABOUT THE AUTHOR

Salvatore Iaquinta is a surgeon in the San Francisco Bay Area. He is a columnist for the Marin Independent Journal. His first book, *The Year They Tried To Kill Me*, is nonfiction. This is his first novel, but borrows heavily from his real-life experiences. He is worshipped by two dogs and merely tolerated by most humans.

ANSWERS TO FREQUENTLY ASKED QUESTIONS:

1. Yes, all the little science-y factoids in the book are true.
2. Yes, I am a nerd.
3. Yes, all the medical stories are true. Sadly.
4. That doesn't surprise me. Email me about it: sneakyelf@hotmail.com
5. Of course, but only on Tuesdays.